# A Legend Awakens

## JH Mull

Copyright © 2024 JH Mull

All rights reserved.

No part of this book may be reproduced, stored in a retrieval system, or transmitted by any means, electronic, mechanical, photocopying, recording, or otherwise, without written permission from the author.

ISBN (Paperback): 979-8-9913611-1-8
ISBN (eBook): 979-8-9913611-0-1

In an era of forgotten optimism where mankind appears to be in an inescapable demise, there is one who is brave enough, one who is cunning enough, and whose destiny will bring hope back to the gloomy crime-ridden Perilous City…

In an era of forgotten optimism where mankind appears to be in an inescapable demise, there is one who is brave enough, one who is cunning enough, and whose destiny will bring hope back to the gloomy crime-ridden Perilous City…

CHAPTER 1

# A Little History

Perilous City is nestled in a valley between the Sierra Nevada mountains and its foothills with the San Joaquin River. A railyard marks its northern and eastern borders with the Sierra Nevada Mountain range as its background. The southern and western-borders are surrounded by many rock cliffs carved from past mining expeditions with only one route through it, a northbound and southbound highway covered by an extensive tunnel hiding several lanes of constant traffic. The skyscrapers have turned this environmental masterpiece into the claustrophobic valley it is today. Because of human intervention, Perilous City is unwelcoming to Mother Nature's wind currents leaving a void of fresh air. It is now the imprisonment of hapless hundreds of thousands of emotionally drained inhabitants.

The dark shadows, cast by immense skyscrapers throughout the metropolis, engulf the streets in an eternal shade of gray, while pollution from below creates a tarnished yellow cloud in continuous suspension above the populace of Perilous City. This blanket of smog creates a shield, trapping the heat radiated by industry and the Sun above making every day a dim and clammy commute. Because of this dreadful atmosphere, there is no wonder why the residents are fearful and accept the anguish brought upon them by the scum who prefer a life of crime and the gift of death.

The normal way of life for the majority has become a challenge of dodging stray bullets and fighting to stay alive. The crime syndicate, Peligrosa, feeds off the deprived inhabitants of Perilous City, while the wealthy residents exist in extravagance on top, hundreds of feet above the downtrodden. This mediocre way of life for the residents is a direct result of when the current mayor cut the police force to a quarter of its size when he took office a decade ago to derail corruption. It is rumored, and like most rumors, based on truth, the Peligrosa work for and are funded by Mayor John Bigler to protect his wealth and votes. This rumor, and Mayor Bigler's family history, have become a normal hostile topic of conversation for the underprivileged citizens of Perilous City. His family's wealth dates to the 1850s when one of his direct ancestors was governor of California.

Like most present occurrences, there is usually a past catalyst in history involved. The catalyst we are referencing has been taught in history classes for almost two hundred years. Well, history classes teach what their government requires them to teach and is so conveniently printed in front of them. Word of mouth has a lot to do with this history as well. What we know from this story is from a little of both…

It was the end of the 1840s and two major occurrences happened within days of one another that would forever change the landscape of California. On the first day, James Marshall was building a sawmill for John Sutter in what is now known as Sacramento. On that day, Mr. Marshall noticed yellow flakes sparkling in a river at the base of the Sierra Nevada Mountains. Within days after James Marshall's "eureka" moment at the now historically famous Sutter's Mill, America gained control of California through the signing of the Treaty of Guadalupe Hidalgo. This treaty ended the

Mexican-American War and gave America a beautiful and bountiful piece of property.

John Sutter and James Marshall tried their best to keep the gold a secret. But, when one arrives in a small town to purchase materials and goods with yellow nuggets, such a secret cannot stay concealed for long. A storekeeper in San Francisco paraded around town with gold that was received in payment from John Sutter. Several months later, miners left San Francisco towards the hills to make fortunes of their own. Excitement grew even more when the president, James Polk, talked about the abundance of gold being excavated from the earth of California. In other words, "There's gold in them there hills!"

When 1849 came to an end, California was admitted to the Union as the 31st state. California's population had grown by the thousands. These new residents came from all over, most from the United States of America and several more from other parts of the world who left their families and hometowns for their chance for unclaimed riches. They mortgaged their homes and lands just to make it rich in sunny California. With the huge influx of population of miners, accommodations needed to be created, and side "Gold Rush" fortunes were shamefully made. Near every established mining camp popped up a saloon, a shop, a brothel, a hotel, and many more side ventures.

It is impossible for a fast-growing population without structure to keep control of crime. As small towns grew so did the lawlessness with gambling, prostitution, and violence. This form of mayhem brought in many criminals. These individuals and gangs wanted to reap the benefits from the discovered wealth. Their idea of becoming wealthy was to murder and rob the miners who were doing all the arduous work.

It has been said, the easiest to obtain, surface gold, in California had greatly vanished by the end of 1850. Another source of mining was desperately needed. At this point, industrialized mining became the prominent form of destroying the landscape just to remove the highly sought-after metal. Larger corporations were formed to manage most of the gold removal. These corporations were more criminalized than the criminals who robbed the mining towns. With the development of hydraulic mining in the early 1850s, enormous profits came pouring in throughout the decade. The drawback with new technology and more riches was regionally ruined landscapes and corruption. With so much gold leaving the state without California making tax revenue on it, the then governor, John Bigler, needed someone to blame.

Finding scapegoats was not going to be difficult. There was a particular set of individuals who were being heralded as heroes in their communities. And heroes are never good for the same government that wants control of their citizens. To make things easier, these five individuals happened to have the same first name, Joaquin. These men had become thorns in the sides of the corrupt businesses and the paid-off government officials. The Five Joaquins, as they were coined, and their gangs were being accused of having committed all the robberies in what was known as the Mother Lode region.

In the early 1850s, the Governor of California, John Bigler, had commissioned a group of individuals known as the California Rangers to capture or kill the Five Joaquins. Surely more than just five people were robbing others. History's perspective of what occurred throughout the Gold Rush is solely based on what is read in the history books. The winning government always writes the history books, and the government has always and will always be in control by the rich and powerful. It's the legends and the tales that are passed on from generation to generation that will always put another twist on the truth taught in schools.

Albeit the roots of this legend are embedded during the California Gold Rush our tale begins seven generations later…

*A Legend Awakens*

High above the stench of poverty and living in a world of his own, the mayor of present-day Perilous City, John Bigler, lives alone in his penthouse on the top floor of the tallest building in the direct center of the city. He's a large individual in all terms of the word. John lives large with riches everywhere. He is 5' 10" weighing close to three hundred pounds with a lot more weight due to food intake instead of exercise. John has a very comforting face. A face that one thinks Santa Clause would look like without his beard. His dark hair is never out of place, probably because it is assumed to be a wig. He's in his fifties and looks his age. John knows no boundaries and overspends on everything. Mayor Bigler, being quite boisterous and arrogant, feels everybody in his city should worship him and be happy that he oversees their lives.

This is John Bigler's penthouse. His family fortune has paid for it. It is a 4,000-square-foot penthouse with an undisclosed number of rooms. Many secrets are held in his home. The penthouse has a balcony with sound-absorbing windows encompassing the entire penthouse giving him and only him what he believes is an unobstructed view of the entire city. John's delusions of grandeur help him believe that he knows what everyone is doing all the time in his city. John's balcony goes around the entire floor, but he has never stepped foot onto it. He is deathly afraid of heights which is directly related to him being afraid of falling from power. Just imagine where his mindset would go if he stepped onto the balcony and finally realized the intense smog blocks his view of everything below him. With his warped thinking, learning he can't see the residents below, probably wouldn't scathe him. He is too engulfed in himself and his inherited status. John has an unhealthy pride in his ancestral heritage.

Mayor Bigler's pride in his family's history is obvious. He has decorated the penthouse with solid gold-framed articles regarding his ancestors, the Gold Rush, and even articles about the Five Joaquins. The furniture looks like they have never been sat in. The only room that his guests see is his office. The office looks like a mini museum with gold trinkets and knick-knacks embellishing the shelves. There is a large painting of the mayor himself greeting the guests as they enter his office. Due to his connection with the Gold Rush, Mayor Bigler feels all the gold that was stolen during his ancestor's reign belongs to him. Right now, the mayor is impatiently pacing back and forth constantly looking at his gold watch saying, "Soon… very soon. Anytime now… anytime…"

CHAPTER 2

# THE STRAW THAT BREAKS THE CAMEL'S BACK

Through the stink of pollution, there is a place, a beacon of solitude and warmth for some and the home to one...
   It's the middle of a typical drab week, just past 6 pm, there is a tiny Mexican diner, Alejandro's, on the south side of 29th Street, open and always ready for customers. Like most businesses at ground level this time of night throughout Perilous City, it's mostly vacant. There is only one customer here tonight. The diner is on a block where the buildings are a uniform five stories tall. Alejandro's is on the first floor; the proprietor, who is the establishment's namesake, owns the building and lives on the second floor. The remaining floors are vacant. Down in the diner, the only audible chatter is behind the counter on the television from the evening news broadcast, "...and that is the seventh drive-by shooting this month—"
   A young soft voice speaks out, "Alejandro, would you please turn that garbage off." There is a young lady sitting on one of the colorful stools resting her elbows on the equally colorful mosaic-tiled countertop. The dozen four-seated tables match the counter

in color only. Each tabletop is solid color alternating in festive reds, oranges, and yellows. The earthtone woods that add structure to the diner bring a feeling of antiquity to the establishment. Tired of the distraught message she is hearing on television, the only client in the diner shakes her head and interrupts the broadcast, "I've had enough of the news. My God, it's the third of the month and there have been seven shootings!" Josefina Murrieta is a very young woman of Mexican descent with long black hair pulled back into a bushy ponytail. She is all dressed in dark workout attire. Her story is the one we will hear for years to come… but not in the history books.

Alejandro, an average-sized American of Mexican descent with a slender stature, as already mentioned, is the proprietor of this diner. It is his pride and joy. And you can tell. He keeps it clean and the ambiance festive. Just like his only customer tonight, Alejandro has a sad story to tell. But unlike his customer, we may never know his complete story. All that is known to us now is he lives above the diner alone with his unshared memories. Alejandro believes strongly in his Mexican heritage and displays it with honor. Although he is a perfect stranger to us, one does feel comfortable with him. He's like a fatherly mentor who makes you feel safe and secure. We don't know his age, but we can see years of wisdom in his eyes. With this knowledge, he tries his best to respond to his seemingly disturbed customer. "You know the reason for that, Josefina…" Alejandro starts lecturing, "Nadie wants to help their community anymore. We, as citizens of our beautiful city, need to keep joy in our corazones and it is our duty to help. La policía are doing all they can but they're outnumbered and not respected."

Josefina humbly interjects, "Respect is earned."

Alejandro picks up the remote and turns down the volume on the television playing in the kitchen. He hobbles with a limp in every other step towards the stereo and starts playing his favorite

Mexican music softly, "I know how you feel about them, but not all are corrupt."

"Shit! You didn't lose your family like I did!"

"Bonita, I will not have you speaking like that in mi cocina!" Alejandro is very stern in his speech at first then settles down to his normal calm tone, "You don't know everything. The problem with children today is that they **think** they know. You're all ignorant. You speak without thought."

"I'm sorry Alejandro. I didn't mean to disrespect you. I'm here every night after I get done at the gym, you always cook me a fantastic meal and all I do is vent my anger to you. I'm tired of seeing everybody so unhappy."

Alejandro, with an everlasting smile and jubilant attitude despite his handicapped walk asks his customer, "Do I look unhappy to you? Trust me, I have a lot to be unhappy about, but I choose to believe that good is still aquí."

"That's why I come here every night. Your diner," Josefina flips her hands and gestures through the air and continues, "your lovely diner is an oasis in this hellhole. It gives me the energy to believe in something and to brave my trek home. Gracias Alejandro, muchas gracias."

"De nada, bonita." Alejandro commences with closing his diner.

Josefina enjoys the rest of her meal with the tranquil sounds of her Hispanic heritage playing in the background. She knows if she waits too long to head home, the streets will be unsafe, becoming populated with the Peligrosa. Josefina grabs her backpack, pays for her meal, and gives Alejandro a quick hug and peck on the cheek as she heads for the door.

Alejandro is quick to offer, "You know if you wait a few minutes, I can walk you home.

"No, I'm good. Thank you anyways." as per her usual, Josefina declines Alejandro's offer to walk her home. Alejandro locks the door behind her then heads to the back of the restaurant turning off the lights.

Once she is on the sidewalk, Josefina faces east and heads towards her home many blocks away from the center of the now dark city. Josefina thinks about waving down a taxi. There are enough streetlights and enough traffic she figures she'll be fine. She clinches a black piece of metal that is attached to a necklace adorned around her neck. Josefina believes this worn piece of metal is her talisman since it has been with her from the night she woke up in the hospital many years before. Josefina continues her walk home. The tall dark buildings dwarf this petite young lady. She is so fragile looking amongst the rest of the residents. During the day she is easily overlooked by most street dwellers. Nighttime, on the other hand, is another story.

There are a few hidden alleyways the residents on the streets of Perilous City use as shortcuts from one street to the next, which are usually devoid of the Peligrosa. The destitute live on these alleyways in makeshift cardboard shacks. No money in their pockets so no interference from the Peligrosa. As a young and very attractive woman walking alone, a wrong turn down one of the alleyways can prove to be treacherous. Josefina approaches one of those alleyways and stands there for several moments thinking. *My apartment's five minutes away if I go that way.* Then she looks down the street she is currently on and continues thinking. *Traffic is slowing down. The police station is on the other side. Around the corner is a church. This way will take about twenty minutes to get home. I shouldn't be scared. I will be brave, stand tall, and walk through **my** city. I've been practicing karate for ten years since my family was taken away from me. I can take care of myself. I will remain confident. I will do this.* Josefina stands tall (as tall as a 5' 4" woman can stand), checks her backpack for the asp (a gift Alejandro had given her when she first stepped into his diner), grasps her necklace tightly, passes the alleyway and continues up the street.

As Josefina heads to the end of the street she looks around and sees the all too familiar Peligrosa insignia graphitized everywhere. The façade of every building has some form of blemish; be it a broken or cracked window, bullet holes in the red brick, or broken railings. With a sigh she thinks, *Alejandro's right, there must still be good here. This city could be rejuvenated. There must be something we can do. I want to do something but what?* Josefina ponders more, thinking of ways she could possibly motivate others to start a neighborhood watch program. Maybe even clean the graffiti and fill in the bullet holes. Because of the over-heaping trashcans, the city streets are quite filthy with garbage sitting on the ground. Every step needs to be watched because stray dogs and cats defecate everywhere. It's quite a dirty city. The pride of the residents has gone, and it's a shame. There was a time this community was beautiful with parks and green trees on top of the hills and throughout the valley.

Josefina's walk down the gloomy block comes to an end rather quickly. The normal activities are occurring; pedestrians rushing out of buildings and getting into their cars, men hollering sexual innuendos out the windows as she passes by, and even the police station has a couple of patrol cars in motion in response to some form of crime somewhere.

Josefina turns the corner and is ten minutes walking distance away from her apartment. She undoes her ponytail, which looks like a black fox's tail, to let down her long black hair. As she runs her fingers through her hair to massage her scalp she glances towards her community church, La Santa Maria. This, not-so-modest mini cathedral, is built with thirty-foot tall walls made of unfinished coarse granite shipped from Pennsylvania between 1849 and 1852. This unfinished granite gives Santa Maria a rough appearance adding to her beauty and charm. The church sits on a base of finished smooth granite that has twelve tiers of steps leading to Santa Maria's two massive twelve-foot doors made of redwood trees.

Equal in height, starting ten feet above the ground where the stairs meet them. The front of the church has four stained glass windows. The two sides of the church have identical-sized stained-glass windows of four each. These twelve windows have a rendering of one of Jesus' disciples. The steeple of the church towers another forty feet into the air topped off with a rather large belltower. When the construction was completed, by some miracle, a large cross of pure gold was donated to the church. It is rumored that the Robin Hood of El Dorado brought it there to give riches back to the poor who had been wrongly taken from them by the corporations that used slave labor to dig for the gold.

The beauty of this church is not what caught Josefina's eyes this moment; there is light radiating from the stained glass windows and there is a black van parked in front of the granite steps. She notices a rough-looking bald man in the driver's seat sporting a Peligrosa tattoo on his forehead, but he is asleep. Josefina is overwhelmed with a feeling of disgust and hatred looking at this individual. She's very skeptical about this situation. She doesn't see anyone else parked around the church. Josefina, therefore, assumes there are no church services tonight, so curiosity overwhelms her. She quietly and quickly darts up the steps towards the large wooden cathedral doors.

With a slight nudge on one of the doors, realizing they are not locked, Josefina continues to muscle the massive door open. This is the first time Josefina has stepped foot into this church. She is quickly thrown back by how large and beautiful it is. There are statues of Biblical saints near the wooden pillars and murals of Biblical stories hung on the walls. The outrageously tall ceiling is painted with scenes representing the Stations of the Cross. The works of Michelangelo in the Sistine Chapel only surpass its beauty. The pillars, pews, window frames, and all the trim are made from matching redwood that the doors are made from. Josefina is in complete admiration of the beauty and possible price tag for

*A Legend Awakens*

the construction of Santa Maria. She is so mesmerized by its massively beautiful design. The only thing that snaps her out of this awe-inspiring sight is hearing some intense arguing coming from the pulpit.

With a deep Irish accent, the grief-stricken priest aggressively and apprehensively pleads, "No, that belongs to the church. It's almost two hundred years old! Haven't you hoodlums taken enough from us?"

Josefina hunches down and creeps further in and sees the church's priest struggling to break free from the clutches of two thugs. Three other hooligans are wrestling with a large gold cross while strapping it to a handcart.

A sixth thug smacks the priest across the face while informing him, "Well, Father, this gold doesn't belong to you anymore. It belongs to someone else and he's paying us dearly for it." The sixth one, fed up with the struggling priest, takes the butt of his gun and strikes him over his head sending him to the ground.

Watching the priest get manhandled burns a fire deep inside Josefina. The thought of getting the police never comes to her mind. Josefina, who is hiding behind the back pew, becomes outraged and fumbles through her backpack to retrieve the asp. Once the asp is tightly in her grasp, she whips it hard, so it fully extends with a loud clank. By pure luck, the noise the asp made was muffled by the clumsy burglars. There is an overwhelming sense of justice pouring through her veins. The three thieves struggling with the solid gold cross are now wheeling the bounty towards the front door. As they approach the last pew, Josefina springs up and with a—CRACK opens the skull of the first thief who instantly loses control of the hand truck.

The splattered blood, which squirted from the cracked skull, found its canvas on Josefina's face. Her hair is now wrapped around her face sticking in place by the intruder's blood. The other two thieves become instantly distracted and can no longer hold on to the handcart to balance the heavy cross. This instability causes it to wobble and lean one way to fall. It pins the second burglar to the ground instantly crushing him. The four remaining thieves and Josefina stand motionless in shock wondering what had just occurred.

Quickly gaining her composure back, Josefina, with adrenaline on her side, lunges forward at the third man who was helping with the cross. Her asp slams down hard on his right shoulder breaking the man's clavicle while instantly knocking his arm out of the socket. Josefina lands on top of him and after a few quick strikes and audible sounds of bones crunching in his face, the third thief becomes immobilized. As quickly as she pounced on top of him, she instinctively dives behind another pew. And it's a good thing she does. The Peligrosa who knocked out the priest starts unloading his gun toward her direction.

After eight loud shots, he yells out to her, "Come out come out wherever you are! I've always wanted to say that." the man chuckles then looks at his two remaining buddies and waves with his empty gun for one crony to go one way and the other to go around the backside. He releases the empty magazine onto the floor and places another one in the gun. "We have you surrounded. You should make it easy on yourself and come out now before I get angry." He chuckles again and says, "That was impressive, we can use a girl like you."

While the criminal was unloading his eight rounds into the pews, Josefina already scurried around to the other side of the church moving fast sliding on the intensely buffed marbled church floor under the pews with her heart racing with excitement. Although Josefina knows she should be scared, she is most certainly enjoying this confrontation. Especially since she noticed the tattoo on the forehead of the man who is trapped under the cross. It is the mark of the Peligrosa, the same tattoo on the man sleeping in the van.

The tattoo is incredibly detailed for being so small. It's the size of a half-dollar. It is a white skull resting inside the coils of a tan rattlesnake with the red, black widow's mark on the skull's forehead. It matches most of the graffiti on the walls of every building in Perilous City. It is the mark Josefina sees every night when she falls asleep. This was the mark on the foreheads of the intruders that killed her family. These tattoos are discreetly hidden from normal view. They are inked on the hairline in the center of the forehead and most of the gang members who have this Peligrosa marking have bangs covering them. Josefina's happiness in killing the Peligrosa is inflamed by the hatred she feels for them. She is finally getting some revenge.

Josefina angrily and confidently replies, "A girl like me! A Peligrosa, me a Peligrosa... I would rather be dead!" No sooner does she reply to him, than she hears someone running her way.

From under the pew, she can see the legs of another Peligrosa. Josefina slides out, swings her right leg around, and trips the fourth Peligrosa face-first on the ground. He hits so hard that he loses the grip on his gun and watches it slide into the side aisle. As he scrambles to get back to his feet, which is not much of a distance for this small-stature man, he turns his head and sees Josefina's asp enter his eye socket. The now one-eyed Peligrosa scampers, trips, gets back to his feet and runs in agony out of the church with the asp sticking out of his face. *Two left* she thinks with a sly smirk. Josefina sees the gun in the aisle and scurries for it.

With the gun in her hand, she jumps up, turns around, and is now looking at the other two Peligrosa in their faces. They are standing on the other side of the pews. Josefina points and shoots eight times. She becomes easily startled at the fact she missed... both of them. Despite this, Josefina throws the gun in their direction as they open fire at her. A split millisecond before they started shooting her reflexes helped her dive to the ground again. Instead of heading towards the door, Josefina slides under the pews towards the pulpit.

Josefina needs something to defend herself with so she grabs two candlestick holders. The two remaining Peligrosa unleashed a few more rounds at Josefina while running in her direction they split to cut her off. Josefina darts behind the pulpit and hides there, breathing heavily, trying to plan her next attack. A couple seconds later the two remaining Peligrosa pop out on each side with their guns facing her. "Now, now little one, aren't we cunning as a fox? The offer still stands. We could use you. You would make a great addition to the team. Heck, we don't mind what you just did to the others. It's impressive is what it is. You would be all of our favorite girl."

Josefina rises slowly with her back against the pulpit standing at five and a half feet tall with her sneakers on. She coyly smiles and informs them while heavily breathing, "I said... I would rather... be... dead."

The sixth Peligrosa points his gun directly at Josefina's head, smiles, and says, "Sorry to hear that, but more than happy to oblige,"—THUNK!

Before he has a chance to pull the trigger the priest smashes him in the back of the head with another candlestick. The last remaining hoodlum swings his gun back and forth between the priest and Josefina trying to decide whom to off first. Before he is able to make his decision Josefina smashes both of the candlesticks she is holding like two cymbals to the sides of his head. The last Peligrosa falls backward slamming himself on top of the marble floor. The priest turns to his savior, drops to his knees, grabs her hands, and kisses them saying, "Thank you child, the church, and this community owe you our gratitude." Then in a worried tone says, "My child you've been shot..."

Josefina replies, "No, I'm fine Father." She looks around and she too notices her left sleeve now has a hole in it and the immediate surrounding area is soaked in blood. Right then she feels some intense pain in her left forearm. Apparently one of the bullets caught her as she hid for safety. "Oh, Father I have to go." Josefina turns to leave.

The priest grabs her right arm and tries stopping her, "You need to go to the hospital. Let me call for help."

Police sirens are now audible from the distance. With apprehension, Josefina sees the flicker of blue and red lights bouncing off the stained glass. "I can't stay. I don't trust them. I've got to go. Is there a back door? Please don't let anyone know I was here."

The father doesn't recognize her. And with Josefina's face full of blood and hair he doesn't think anyone would recognize her. He does, however, recognize the urgency in her eyes and points to the back of the church. Josefina nods her head in thanks and darts out towards the back alley. As she abruptly leaves, the police enter the church with guns drawn.

CHAPTER 3

# CAPTAIN AND CRIMINAL

For the past ten years, no one in Perilous City has ever stood their ground with the Peligrosa. Let alone stop them from committing a crime. Therefore, it should not come as a mystery as to why the press and the Channel Six News crew are scurrying outside the perimeter of yellow crime scene tape surrounding Santa Maria. All the floodlights brightly light up the street. An observer from a distance would see total chaos with the commotion of police, paramedics, and journalists scampering around. The residents are out of their apartments watching and wondering in awe, a rare occurrence… especially at night.

The lead anchor of the six o'clock news, Mercedes Downey, is here to report. She is an attractive woman dressed very professionally. Mercedes is standing next to a tall handsome individual with half a week's worth of beard stubble who would rather be somewhere else. Mercedes' cameraperson tells her, "We're live in five, four, three...," then motions with his fingers two and one and points at her.

"Hello and good evening Perilous City, this is Mercedes Downey with a special report reporting for News Channel Six, I'm here with Captain Harry Love of the Perilous City Police Force.

*A Legend Awakens*

It is our understanding that an unknown hero has foiled a robbery attempt. Captain Love, please let our viewers know what happened tonight."

Captain Love takes a strong posture and composes himself professionally before he speaks, "Well, Mercedes, I can't get into too many details at this moment, but there was an alleged robbery attempt."

Mercedes is hoping for more, but Captain Love keeps silent. "Well then, Captain Love, how many perpetrators from the Peligrosa gang were involved?"

The captain sneers with an apprehensive grin and answers, "There is no confirmation that the Peligrosa are behind this, we have been told there were six intruders involved and we have three in custody."

"Three in custody?!? Did the other three get away?"

The captain, trying not to feed into anything and definitely not enjoying the camera in his face, "One is still at large while two were found nonresponsive at the scene."

Mercedes, excitement is very noticeable because she is the only news anchor with this exclusive story. She has a captive audience, "Do you know who stopped the burglary? Was anyone else involved?"

"Well, Mercedes, we only have one eyewitness, Father O'Riley. He told us in our initial interview that an angel from 'Heaven' saved him and the church. That's all for now Mercedes. I'll be holding a press conference tomorrow evening." Captain Love removes the microphone from his shirt, hands it to Mercedes, and leaves the view of the camera.

Mercedes ends her short interview with a monologue to the camera, "Well Perilous City residents, it appears someone is looking over us tonight. Please stay tuned to Channel Six News so we can keep you informed when more details arrive. Make sure to watch tomorrow's six o'clock evening news. This is Mercedes Downey with a special report reporting for Channel Six News."

In the center of Perilous City, at One Bigler Avenue, on the top floor in the penthouse high above, John Bigler loses his temper and becomes very erratic. His constant heavy-footed stomping and pacing back and forth is only demeaned by his red sweaty face and froth of spit coming from the sides of his mouth. He starts throwing a tantrum by swiping his arms across a few stands within his reach knocking the gold trinkets to the ground and pounding his fist on the walls. John just finished watching the Channel Six News and exclaims, "Turn that God damn thing off! What do you mean a defenseless girl stopped six men with guns?" Mayor Bigler has company, Ricardo, his main henchman, a very sleazy individual with no morals. Ricardo oversees the Peligrosa. He and his gang live rent-free in an "abandoned" building at the railyard on the north side of town.

Ricardo, in his raspy chain-cigarette-smoking-induced voice without any emotion says, "I'm sorry Mr. Bigler sir. That's what I got out of William before he passed out."

With an exhausted pant from his childish outrage, the mayor calms down and asks, "Yes, yes, William, how is he doing?"

Keeping his same posture with a lit cigarette dangling from his lips, Ricardo proceeds to answer, "Well sir, you see, he lost a lot of blood with the loss of his eye and all—"

Switching emotions instantly, Mayor Bigler snaps, "I DON'T GIVE A FLYING MONKEY'S ASS ABOUT HIM! I WANT MY GOLD CROSS! Do you know how hard I have worked to get all my ancestors' gold back?! Tell me Ricardo, where were you when all this was happening?"

Remembering all too well his startling disturbance of sleep when William opened the van door earlier that night, he tells the mayor, "I was in the van keeping a lookout for the police."

"Damn you! I own the police! Well, the corrupt ones. I own most of the police!" Mayor Bigler smacks a few more gilded knick-knacks in Ricardo's direction, "While you were keeping an eye on the police a little girl snuck by you. What do you have to say for yourself?"

Ricardo has caught several of the gold objects that were thrown at him. He discreetly hides them in his leather vest pockets while the mayor stomps around. Lips holding tight to his cigarette, he says with a lopsided smile, "I'm sorry—"

Mayor Bigler interrupts Ricardo again and in a very condescending manner retorts, "I'm sorry sir, I'm sorry sir. I'm sick and tired of excuses! I want results! Get out of here! Get me, Captain Love. I need him at my office right away!"

Ricardo, proud of being in charge of the Peligrosa, has a completely shaven head with a Peligrosa tattoo prominently showing as he rides his favorite mode of transportation, his vintage Indian motorcycle, through the city streets. Everyone moves out of his way fearing they will become a target of distress. No one looks him in the eyes. Ricardo wears a clichéd biker-gang outfit with a leather vest, black jeans, and chains for décor, quite a stupid spectacle. He is tan-skinned with several piercings on his nose, ears, and lower lip. He can always be seen mumbling something. Taking advantage of anyone afraid of him is his specialty. He dishes out violence and pain to anyone he wants. The fake acting of being cordial with the mayor will only go so far with him. No one knows where his deep hatred for mankind comes from. Living, for Ricardo, is a life of fighting and drinking and everything that goes with that choice of lifestyle. After a few hours of drinking with his Peligrosa gang at the railyard, Ricardo remembers to continue the mission Mayor Bigler put forth: find Captain Love and tell him to see the mayor.

Riding his beloved Indian with a loud motorcycle roar, Ricardo pulls up to Captain Love's apartment complex. This side of the city very rarely sees the Peligrosa because of the poverty. Captain

Love's building should be condemned. At least Harry doesn't live on the top floor... he won't have to worry about leaks. Ricardo revs the throttle several times, waking the rest of the residents before turning off the motorcycle and dismounting.

Harry Love hears the commotion on the street, "What now? I just got to bed." He tiredly lifts himself out of bed and places both feet on the floor. Dirty clothes are spread all over the one-room apartment. Dressed only in his tighty-whities, Harry heads to the window while his bed flops back into the wall. He shakes his head in disgust at his living conditions. A one-burner stove and a mini fridge are his only appliances. One would think a captain's salary would go further in a city with two million residents. Not when one has been married twice and has two children with each ex-wife. Looking out the window, he sees Ricardo standing on the street below smoking a cigarette and pressing the buzzer. Harry opens the window and whispers down, "You're a dumb ass. How many times do I have to tell you that buzzer doesn't work? And I don't want you coming here. Reputation you know."

Ricardo looks up with a yellow smile disrupted by a couple of missing teeth and says to Harry, "Your reputation, fine Captain, is as good as mine. You're no better than I am. Captain, Mr. Big wants you." Ricardo flicks his cigarette up towards the second-story window. He flips Harry the bird, mounts his bike, and drives off with a ton of commotion.

Being summoned to the mayor's office by a common thug, one that he should be putting into jail, embarrasses Harry Love, Captain of the Perilous City police force. Harry jostles with the window and shuts it with a little fight. Very depressed with his situation, Harry goes to the refrigerator, grabs the orange juice, and mixes it with some vodka. He tops it off with some blue curaçao to make a moldy screwdriver. He then sets it on his nightstand. Harry pulls down his bed and quickly jumps on it before it flips up again. He sits crossed-legged in the middle of the bed and reaches over to his nightstand grabbing his drink. With no hesitation, he swallows the moldy screwdriver in one large gulp. He wipes his mouth with his right arm and puts the glass back on the nightstand. Harry flops back and stares blankly at the cracked ceiling listening to the rats rummaging on the floor.

CHAPTER 4

# BREAKFAST

Across the street from One Bigler Avenue is Two Bigler Avenue, the Perilous City government building, where the mayor's office is located. It is not your typical government building with white columns and gold domes. This building looks more like a prison. There are guards posted at every entrance with barbed razor wire surrounding the windows. It is a ten-story building taking up one block. Just like the building across the road, the top floor has one resident. The mayor's office is almost a replica of his penthouse's office. The major difference is the mayor's office is brighter and doesn't have a mysterious cabinet in the far corner. What ties it to the penthouse is the amount of gold items on stands and historical relics hanging on the walls.

John is now in his office sitting at his enormous desk enjoying a hearty breakfast when Harry walks in. John excitedly smiles and welcomes the captain, "Hello and good morning, Captain Love, what brings you here so early? Don't you have a press conference to prepare for?"

Stern and authoritative, Harry Love answers, "Very funny John, you know why I'm here, you sent your goon to fetch me. I don't appreciate you sending that scum. You know I can't stand him or

*A Legend Awakens*

his uncanny methods. I have a reputation to maintain. I can't be seen with the Peligrosa. So do me a favor, stop sending him. I can be reached on my cellphone. You still have the number, John?"

Childish and unaware, John demands, "First of all, I am your mayor, so please call me so... It's respect. I respect your title and call you captain. Is it so hard to call me mayor? Second, sending Ricardo is fun. It keeps you on your toes. And third... we have a problem. Did you see this morning's paper?"

Harry ignoring John's ranting about respect asks, "What the hell does the paper have to do with it? I have bigger issues to deal with."

"Your issues deal directly with this gibberish." John tosses the paper to Harry. "Here, read the article in this morning's paper."

***Two Peligrosa perish in a religious raid: The city champions a new hero.***

*By: Rea Peterman*

*Father O'Riley was doing his routine rounds when he heard some suspicious activities coming from the front of La Santa Maria. He reported six Peligrosa were attempting to steal the 175-yea-old Solid Gold ½ ton Cross. He tried to talk them out of what they were doing by quoting the scriptures, but it was to no avail. He was knocked down by one of the Peligrosa. Father O'Riley said it was a miracle his church was saved. When he awoke the bandits were all unconscious. The police did arrive late, like usual, to find two Peligrosa dead and three incomprehensible. The Sixth is still at large. Father O'Riley not knowing which angel saved him said, "The blessed angel will always be in my prayers."*

> *We congratulate this unknown hero and like all citizens of Perilous City, we hope for the best in all you do. This paper does not approve of vigilantism. If they plan to come back to finish the job they need to think twice. A generous donation was given to the church to have a state-of-the-art security system installed. Continued on B-5*

Harry glances over the article and plops it back on the mayor's desk then sits down, "So who cares? Murders happen all the time since you took office. This story will be forgotten later today."

"Of course, I want this act of heroism forgotten, but what if no one forgets it and others do the same."

"You think the public wants to revolt? They probably do… but that is why your Peligrosa keeps them in line."

The mayor continues shoveling his mouth with toast, bacon, and eggs. After he swallows chunks of food and gulps down orange juice, the mayor climbs from his desk. John struggles with his girdle trying to make his three hundred pounds look like two hundred. Captain Love shakes his head because it isn't working. The mayor finishes off by tucking his shirt back in and buttoning his black suit jacket. He wipes his mouth on a napkin tossing it aside on his desk. "Now, listen Captain, I want that woman found. William saw her but isn't able to tell us what she looks like. He didn't get a good take on her. She slammed something into his eye. The physician is tending to him now. I'm six men down! She singlehandedly took out Rico by busting his skull wide open. That gold cross, which should be mine, crushed Sammy. He suffocated under that thing. One idiot has a broken shoulder and can't speak because his jaw is wired shut and he's at the city hospital under lock and key. My two other goons are locked up in your jail right now with broken skulls or amnesia or something."

*A Legend Awakens*

Captain Harry Love interjects, "I just can't release them. They were caught with their hands in the cookie jar. Father O'Riley makes quite a strong witness. Besides they tried stealing La Santa Maria's cross."

Going insane John flips, "No! No! That gold is mine! Let those two pinheads stay there all I care! If a girl can beat them, why would I want them in my organization anyways! They fear me more than they fear your poor excuse of a jail!"

Rolling his eyes regarding the 'poor excuse of a jail' remark, Harry mumbles to himself, "No thanks to you."

"What was that?"

"Nothing, please continue."

"I want this woman found. Let's treat her like a hero. The city wants one, let's give them one. I will offer her the 'key' to the city. Get Father O'Riley to the podium with you this afternoon. Convince him of the importance of finding her. With him pleading to the public with a description, we are sure to get her. Once out in the open, we'll have the Peligrosa take care of her, and everything will go back to normal."

"I tried getting a description out of him last evening, but O'Riley said he was unconscious through the whole thing. That's where I don't believe him. When my men entered the church, they said he was standing and alert. He was looking at the back door where my men found a blood trail that disappeared in the dumpster. He's saying it must be an angel."

"If you can't get the description, I'm sure Ricardo can."

"Please don't send Ricardo. I'll convince O'Riley."

"I will be watching at six o'clock tonight. And Captain, if he's not on it I will have Ricardo visit him."

"Ricardo won't be necessary. We have her blood. I will have the results by tomorrow. Remember as a citizen of Perilous City everyone here will have their DNA on record."

The mayor looks with skepticism, "Yeah… right, everyone. That's if they were born here or legally moved here. I'm in the system and you are, but we know a lot of people in common that the system forgot."

Captain Love rises from the chair and proceeds to leave. Harry points at his own mustache and says to John, "Oh, and John, you have some egg right there." Then he closes the door. With a big smile, he hears John scream, "MAYOR!!! CALL ME MAYOR!!!"

## CHAPTER 5

# A SAD PAST

Before all the press and the Channel Six News crew were hounding the church and before the police had any clue as to what was happening, Josefina had just made it out the backdoor of the church. She glances to the right towards the street where she can see the flashing police lights and then looks left towards the dumpsters. There is a fire escape on the building adjacent to the church. Josefina hustles to the first dumpster, reaches in and grabs a garbage bag. She empties the smelly garbage from the bag into the bin and places it over her left arm to stop the dripping blood trail. She thinks, *damn it, my blood is in the church.* Josefina has the right to be concerned. When she was twelve years old her DNA was put into the city's database. The theory behind this DNA mapping of the city's residents was to promote safety and well-being. Most residents didn't know this had happened, but a few did. Josefina is one of the few who knew… it was just by chance though…

Ten years ago, a week after the mayoral election, the Murrieta family was hosting a huge family gathering at their beautiful home. This dwelling was built sometime before the turn of the twentieth century and resided within the Perilous City limits at the edge of a park. It was a rather large home; some may even have called it a mansion. Rich they were not, but the Murrieta's had owned the home since it was erected. The middle-class Murrieta's worked hard for what they had. All the furniture was made around the same time the house was built. What the house looked like really doesn't matter. What mattered then was that the entire Murrieta family was there; brothers, sisters, aunts, uncles, cousins, everyone. The then twelve-year-old Josefina was the youngest of the Murrietas and she, like the others, were bowing their heads in silence preparing to give thanks for their meal. No sooner did the family say grace, did a bunch of hoodlums break down the door and start shooting the family and pillaging the home. Josefina quickly ran for cover between two dining room hutches and watched the intruders kill her family.

The Peligrosa had broken into her home looking for money, jewelry, and all types of metals. They kept demanding the gold. Josefina's older brother Antonio grabbed his little sister and tried to bring her to safety. She watched one of the Peligrosa riding her brother's dark black motorcycle right into the foyer. The man on the bike got off and jumped in front of them.

Antonio, while holding onto his little sister, swung with his left hand and knocked several teeth out of the Peligrosa's mouth. Josefina watched him fly backward onto her brother's bike. The tattoo of a white skull with a red, black widow's mark on the head nestled in the coils of a tan rattlesnake was embedded into the twelve-year-old's mind. Antonio, while holding his sister Josefina, was taking a beating. While absorbing a few hits with metal pipes, chains, and a couple of bullets, Antonio managed to fall down the basement stairs while holding his sister safely in his arms.

The Peligrosa poured gasoline all over the upstairs and set fire to the three-story home. Antonio placed Josefina on top of the icebox and told her to stay there. He ran up the basement stairs only to find it impossible to open the door. Smoke started pouring in from the bottom of the door. He tried several times to bust the

*A Legend Awakens*

door down, but something was pinned against it. The Peligrosa was going to have them burn alive. He had to think fast. This home was one of the original homes built back in the late 1800s and was made mostly of wood with some brick reinforcements. Antonio ran back to his sister and lifted the crying child from the icebox. He opened it and started hurling the food out. He explained to his sister that she needed to be very calm and not to breathe heavily. He unplugged the box, wrapped his thick shirt around her, and placed her in it. Antonio remained very calm when he told his sister as he closed the door, "Josefina, be brave and strong. Stay in here as long as you can. This will protect you from the flames. Breathe slowly and take small breaths. Don't worry about me. I'll be fine." Antonio gave his sister one last kiss on her forehead and then continued, "Remember the family legacy." He shut the door just in time as the floors above caved in.

After the fire was extinguished and with a few smoldering timbers left, a close-to-retirement county sheriff's deputy walked along the rubble and found a burnt corpse protecting an icebox. He thought that was strange and immediately disturbed the crime scene by pushing the charred corpse off the freezer and opened the lid. To his surprise, there was a little girl barely alive in it. He reached in and grasped her tightly into his arms. As he was carrying the cold unconscious girl to safety his leg slipped between some smoldering rafters and snapped his knee. In intense pain, he handed Josefina to a fireman who then took her to the ambulance. The deputy sat himself up and looked at the corpse next to him. It was the burnt corpse that he had pushed aside moments earlier. He noticed that one of the hands was clutching a chain. He snapped the fingers to find a little chunk of gold metal dangling on the end of the chain. He put it in his coat and pulled himself to safety.

The deputy, with crutches, visited the hospital room that Josefina was taken to for recovery. She was sound asleep. He was wearing a cast around his leg and maneuvered around the attending nurse with the crutches quite clumsily. He placed a little box next to her bedside and left. As he was leaving, the deputy asked the nurse if Josefina was all right and she told him she was physically fine. They were just worried about the emotional impact.

Josefina woke up shortly after and overheard the nurse arguing with a doctor about how it wasn't fair that her DNA was going into the system. They had no right to register her DNA into the system without permission. She heard the doctor tell the nurse if she didn't like it, they could take up the issue with the mayor or they could move out of the city.

Josefina ended up in an orphanage with no family to claim her. Although she seemed fine, she knew no one wanted to adopt a child with so much baggage. Living at the orphanage wasn't a horrible situation. The orphanage took great care of her. For years they had enrolled Josefina in self-defense classes, gymnastic classes, fencing classes… anything to keep her mind from wandering. The moment of her eighteenth birthday she left the orphanage and acquired a job as a fitness instructor in a gym next to a Mexican diner on the south side of 29th Street. For the past four years, she has maintained her activities without getting involved in any relationships. She is a loaner and plans on staying that way. She does not want to lose loved ones again, like she had ten years earlier.

CHAPTER 6

# Doctor's Visit

While climbing the emergency escape ladder adjacent to Santa Maria to go home, Josefina quickly reminisces about her sad past and how great it felt to take her aggression out on some of the Peligrosa. She has been bottling her anger for so long. For the first time, she feels alive! In essence, with an adrenaline-induced euphoria, Josefina flies the rest of the way home leaping through the air from one apartment building to the next until she arrives safely at her abode.

Josefina's apartment is at the top floor, and she has no way to enter her apartment because the roof door is locked from the inside. She quickly descends the nine stories by using the fire escape. Although all the apartments have tenants, Josefina passes no one on the way upstairs to her apartment.

She anxiously and apprehensively unlocks the door expecting a Peligrosa or the city police to come after her. Knowing the apartment layout better than any stranger would, Josefina doesn't turn on the lights. She shuts and locks her door and then dashes for the bathroom. After she slams the door behind her, Josefina leans against it, panting then calms herself down. About ten minutes pass and Josefina figures if anyone knew it was her, they would have found her by now. She decides to clean up.

Josefina takes her blood-soaked clothing off and stuffs them into the garbage bag she had around her arm. She tosses the bag off to the side on the tiled floor. She settles herself in with a warm and much-earned bath. She scrubs herself and rinses the gunshot wound with agony until she feels she has comfortably removed all the contaminants from it. Miss Murrieta gets out of the bathtub and places the washcloth on her wound. She then throws her towel on the toilet seat and sits down.

Josefina leans forward and opens the sink cupboard removing her very old first aid kit. Most of the kit is empty. There is, however, a sewing needle in it, minus the thread. Josefina grabs some waxed dental floss and the sewing needle to patch the missing flesh in her lower arm. The bullet knocked a chunk of flesh out of it. There is a lot of blood but after several sloppy-looking stitches, the jagged gap is closed. She decides to tolerate the pain because tonight she is going to be busy. She has no antiseptics. Instead of going to a local drug store, Josefina decides to go to the hospital where she was a patient ten years prior.

At the same time as the Channel Six News interview with Mercedes Downey and Captain Harry Love, Josefina ventures to the hospital. She is very nervous on her trek there because she doesn't want to be caught. Clothed all in black, while carrying the garbage bag, she slips through the streets unseen. Halfway to the hospital, Josefina sees a burning barrel down one of the dark alleyways. She sneaks closer to the only source of light for the alley's residents. A homeless family was having dinner by the barrel. She asks them, "Mind if I burn this." Not waiting for an answer, she drops the garbage bag with the soiled clothing into the fire. Josefina nods at the family, wishes them a safe night and continues to the hospital.

Besides the normal graffiti, there is no sign of the Peligrosa tonight since her earlier run-in with them. Even though she is pumped up to see another one, the realization creeps in, she has nothing to defend herself with. She had watched her asp disappear from the church a couple of hours earlier. It really doesn't matter; all the Peligrosa are off the street and the police are at La Santa Maria. The vacancy of her troubles not patrolling the area does not make her stop flinching whenever a cat hisses or a dog barks as she walks by. Not knowing how much time has passed, Josefina finds herself standing in front of the emergency entrance to the hospital.

Josefina smiles looking at the brightly lit sign, EMERGENCY ENTRANCE, because the hospital is the only public building that has an emergency entrance. Every other public place be it a restaurant, shopping mall, movie theatre, or government building has emergency exits. Distracted with the thought, Josefina walks into the emergency room. After she enters the hospital, she realizes she is wearing the entirely wrong set of clothing. A black pulldown knit hat, black turtleneck, black sweatpants, and black sneakers stick out amongst all the bright white of a disinfected environment. Traveling around a hospital that requires security badges is going to be tougher than she thought. While whispering, *"what was I thinking,"* Josefina backs out of the hospital. She's contemplating how she can gain access to her medical records. She finds herself walking through the parking garage. Josefina notices the medical staff's parking section and goes there to wait.

The stay in the parking garage isn't long. Josefina sits waiting only a few minutes when a BMW comes pulling in. A young doctor climbs out. In a light flirtatious voice, Josefina asks, "Excuse me, are you a doctor?"

"Well, hello…" he says looking her up and down liking what he sees, "What can I do for you?"

"Where is your ID card? How do I know you're a doctor?"

The young doctor opens his jacket, the ID card is pinned to the shirt underneath it. "Do you need help?"

Josefina encroaches on the doctor's personal space and sternly says, "Yes, I actually do need help. I need something to sterilize a wound and my medical records."

The doctor looks a little confused, "Are you hurt? Do you need me to get an orderly?"

Josefina realizes this is not going the way she hoped. She tells the doctor she's sorry then swings with all her might at his chin spinning him around on his BMW. She grabs his keys and pops the trunk open. It takes her a few moments, but she manages to get him into the trunk. She takes his ID card, removes his coat then shuts the trunk. Josefina removes her hat, dons his jacket, takes a deep breath, and heads into the hospital.

Gaining access to the hospital is easier than she thought it would be with someone else's ID. Josefina just holds the ID in front of the scanners and all the doors open for her. She follows the directions to the records room. Once Josefina arrives at the records room acquiring access is simple. Again, the ID lets her in. There is an accounts clerk sitting at one of the computers chatting on the phone with one of her friends. Josefina asks where they keep the physical files of the patients. The lady tells her there are no physical records just computer records. As the lady was talking on the phone she asked, to Josefina seems to be in a manner the accounts clerk is being disturbed, "Whose records do you need?"

Josefina, a little thrown back from the question, thinks, *will it be this easy?* Then asks, "Please, could you pull up Josefina Murrieta's files?"

"How do you spell it?"

"J-O-S-E-F-I-N-A"

Seeming very annoyed the lady says to Josefina, "Yeah, yeah, I know how to spell, Josefina. I need the last name. There are various spellings for it."

Josefina rolling her eyes back at her thinking how she had seen her first name spelled differently many times continues "Okay, that's Murrieta, M-U-R-R-I-E-T-A."

After hitting enter, the accounts clerk said, "No records found," then the lady continued talking on the phone with her friend as she continued typing.

"Can you try the other spellings?"

"I just did. No records found." The lady tells her friend she must go and then with curiosity while she is typing says, "That's weird doctor."

"What's weird?" Josefina inquisitively asks.

"There are no records for any Murrieta... no matter what the spelling. There must be a glitch in the system."

"What type of glitch?"

"Actually, there isn't a glitch. I can't explain it. There are only two ways; someone erased all the data or no Murrietas ever stepped foot into this hospital. Sorry. Do you want me to run any more files? Doctor..." The accounts clerk turns around to finally see the doctor, but Josefina is gone.

Miss Murrieta is completely stunned. If she hadn't seen it with her own eyes, she wouldn't have believed it herself. She saw the accounts clerk typing in every file; birth records, coroner's records, and medical records... no records were found. She began thinking to herself, *Why? My brothers and sisters and my cousins were all born here. My entire family was brought here after their murder. I was brought here after that night. How are there no records?* Josefina heads back to the parking garage totally forgetting about the sterilizer. She jumps back in the BMW, puts her hat back on, and places the doctor's jacket on the seat. She pushes the trunk release button and heads back to the apartment. As Josefina disappears a wobbly and shaken-up doctor climbs out of his trunk holding his sore chin.

CHAPTER 7

# FRIDAY AT LAST

While Josefina tosses and turns trying to sleep all night, the equally disturbed mayor finds it difficult to sleep. When morning arrives, and at the same time Mayor John Bigler is having his breakfast and discussion with Captain Harry Love, Josefina rises from her bed. Her arm is throbbing but manageable. She goes to her bathroom again and pours some mouthwash on the wound and twitches a little. She pulls her hair back into the normal puffy-styled ponytail she usually sports. Josefina decides not to wear black today. Instead, she is out of character wearing white and red workout attire.

Josefina sets off to start the day in her normal manner but this time with more confusion. She takes her regular half-hour walk to work but something is different. Along the way, two people actually said, "good morning," to her. This has never happened before. Josefina is clueless regarding the effect of the domino she knocked down the night before. Life is a thin fine thread and once something pushes against it, a chain reaction occurs. The thread bends and vibrates and sometimes snaps. No matter what, it doesn't remain the same. Josefina will have to take whatever action comes her way now. She didn't just push the thread, she aggressively hit it.

*A Legend Awakens*

Part of her daily walk brings Josefina right by La Santa Maria, the church she had visited the previous evening. As she nonchalantly passes, Josefina sees several police cars and a news van still parked in front of the granite mini cathedral. Josefina tries not to look, but like a cat, curiosity gets the better of her. She glances up to the top of the granite steps and right in front of the massive wooden doors she sees Father O'Riley talking with a tall man. She wonders who this unshaven man, in a slightly unkempt suit, talking with Father O'Riley is. He must be someone of authority since he is on the other side of the yellow crime scene tape. She doesn't know that he is Captain Love. The priest seems very happy waving at everyone as the pedestrians walk by. Father O'Riley then turns away from the captain and enters the church with Harry following him in.

While passing the church, Josefina starts wondering about a ton of different things. She is confused about why her family doesn't exist in the hospital records. This leads her to wonder if it has something to do with the death of her entire family ten years prior. As Josefina turns the corner a loud disturbance drives by. A shifty bald individual with a Peligrosa tattoo on his forehead passes on his very obnoxiously loud and familiar-looking black Indian motorcycle. She stares at him with intense burrowing eyes as if it were an eternity. A lump appears in Josefina's throat. Is this the same bike in her foyer a decade ago? The bike looks like her brother, Antonio's motorcycle. Josefina's raw gut instinct tells her this won't be the last time this Peligrosa, and she would cross paths.

Although Josefina is more exhausted than normal, she makes it to work on time, at ten in the morning. As she enters the employee lounge Josefina notices a more jubilant attitude amongst the employees. Josefina's fellow coworkers are having an inquisitive discussion about the occurrences from the previous night. One of them tosses Josefina the paper and she reads the entire newspaper article about her spoiling the Peligrosa's raid of La Santa Maria. A smirk comes to Josefina's face while reading the article. Apparently, the newspaper approves of what Josefina had done. She hands the newspaper back to her coworker and leaves the room to get ready to teach her first "boot camp" class of the day.

Josefina greets the ten eagerly awaiting gym members who are ready to begin their energetic calorie-burning workout. It is a forty-five-minute class, and she starts it feeling energized. By the end of the intense workout, Josefina feels very weak from her adventure combined with a lack of breakfast. After the class empties, Josefina heads to the employee bathroom and grabs the first aid kit. She changes the dressings on her bullet wound and goes to the now-empty lounge to rest. Josefina stretches out on the couch and closes her eyes.

While Josefina was falling asleep a fellow female coworker entered the lounge, saw her lying there and pranced to the couch sitting on the arm then asked, "Is everything okay Jose?"

Josefina snaps out of her deep comatose rest and while slurping up some drool she asks, "I'm sorry, Krista, did you say something?"

Krista with a motherly concern asks, "Are you alright? Are you feeling well?"

Josefina knows she is physically drained and hopes no one will notice. She can't have medical attention because the bullet wound would need to be reported to the police and she is afraid she will go to jail. "I'm fine. I just had a rough night. Found it hard to sleep. I think I'm coming down with a cold."

"That's unlike you. I have never seen you sick."

"When I walked home last night, I didn't have my jacket zipped all the way."

"You walked home?" Krista seems stunned, especially knowing how unsafe the streets are.

"Yes, it was a nice night, a little chilly out, but I walked home instead."

At that moment Josefina's boss, Cameron, barges in and says with excitement, "You see the news today? Oh, boy… someone took a swing at the Peligrosa. Hey JoJo, isn't that church on your street?"

Josefina, apprehensive at answering and feeling exhausted replies, "It's about three blocks from me," then she continues, "but I didn't hear anything. Living in this city you get accustomed to the sirens and gunshots."

Cameron, in agreement, says, "No kidding. There isn't a day that goes by that someone doesn't get shot in this godforsaken hellhole."

Josefina unsympathetically asks, "Why don't you do something about it?"

"And get myself KILLED! No thanks! Let's not forget how powerful the Peligrosa really are. Even the police do nothing."

Josefina squirms her way to a sitting position carefully not putting any pressure on her left arm. She argumentatively alleges, "That's why we live in fear because people like you won't do anything."

Krista, feeling the tension gets off the arm of the couch and says, "Well my next class is here, I got to go. I hope you feel better." She bounces out avoiding the rest of the conversation.

Her boss asks, "What's wrong? You're not feeling good?"

"Well…' Josefina said correcting his grammar. "I'm just a little under the weather that's all."

"JoJo, I can have someone else cover your shift for you. So, please, feel free to go home." He suggested.

"I'll finish my shift. Thank you though. I just need a quick rest. My next class starts in twenty minutes. I'll be fine."

"Alright, don't forget to watch the news tonight. Mercedes is covering the press conference about the church. She's fine!"

Josefina rolls her eyes, "Sure, I won't miss it."

Josefina does stay to finish her classes, but she switches with a few of the other employees. She teaches Pilates and shows the new members how to use the Nautilus equipment properly. By the time four in the afternoon arrived, Josefina finished her final class. Although she took it relatively easy, she is beyond exhaustion. She somehow gets the strength to clean up with a comforting shower and with the first aid kit, applies more disinfectant to her wound and changes her bandages.

Josefina hasn't eaten anything all day and she knows she needs nourishment to gain strength. When the gym is locked tight, Josefina's boss jumps in his car and drives off while the other employees are going to share a taxi. It's Friday, and Josefina's extremely happy the weekend has arrived. She's off and needs the weekend to recuperate. But first, she needs to refuel. There is only one place for her. She heads for the diner next door, Alejandro's.

A jubilant Alejandro is slicing some vegetables when he sees his favorite customer walking quite gingerly through the door. He greets Josefina as she walks into the diner, "Good afternoon bonita, que pasa?"

An exhausted Josefina answers, "Hola Alejandro, I'm okay and you?"

"Just okay! I thought for sure, you, of all people would be happy with what happened last night. I figure you would be doing summersaults."

Still not sounding ecstatic but smiling she says, "Oh, yes, I'm happy with that. I'm just extremely tired."

An inquisitive Alejandro asks, "Busy day?"

"You can say that."

"I'm sorry, where are my manners? You look hungry. What would you like tonight?"

"Alejandro, I need something to build up some energy. I'll take two chicken fajitas on a plate of your delicious rice with jalapeños and a fresh fruit smoothie please."

*A Legend Awakens*

"I'll tell you what; I'll also make you a bowl of my chili, so you have something tonight when you get home."

With a heartwarming smirk and a very sincere tone of gratitude, Josefina replies, "Te amo, Alejandro. That sounds magnifico."

Josefina's food arrives in time for the news. Alejandro is impressed, besides his regular customer Josefina, the restaurant at this time of day is usually vacant. Today, he actually has three couples in his diner. All day long the diner is busy with customers and usually by five the place sits empty except for Josefina. He asks the customers if they wouldn't mind if he turns down the radio to turn the news on. Everyone is curious about the press conference so there are no objections. The curiosity is more for finding out which brave soul was brave enough to oppose the Peligrosa.

"Hello and good evening Perilous City, this is Mercedes Downey for News Channel Six at six. Last night at eleven, I brought you an exclusive interview with Captain Harry Love…"

On the television set, there is a picture of Captain Love from last night's interview. Josefina recognizes him immediately. It's the tall man with a mustache that she saw earlier this morning on her way to work. He was talking to Father O'Riley when she walked by the church. While Mercedes was talking, Josefina's left arm kept throbbing with every heartbeat. She taps her glass with the fork to get Alejandro's attention. "Alejandro, do you have any painkillers?"

A concerned Alejandro answers, "Yes. Do you have a headache?"

"My head hurts. I also think I may have a fever."

"I'll go get you some." Alejandro proceeds to the kitchen with his missed step limp. A few moments later he comes back with a couple of pain relievers, fever reducers, and a tall glass of water.

With a thumbs up and a smile of gratitude, Josefina thanks him and then swallows the medicine. As the six o'clock news broadcast turns to background noise, Josefina has a disturbing thought. The phonebook at the end of the counter catches her eye. Josefina places her hands on the counter and slowly rises. She walks even slower towards the phonebook with her head cocked slightly towards the left with a pondering countenance. She stands quietly over the phonebook just staring at it. She reaches over with her right arm and starts flipping through the pages.

Josefina moves a handful of pages and passes the C's then grabs a big chunk and flips to the G's then the M's. She starts moving a couple of pages at a time. Ma's, Me's, Mi's, Mo's, then N's. Oops. Josefina flips back a few pages and makes it to the Mu's. Mueller, Mullarny, Murdock, Murrow. She confusedly flips back and forth several times and actually retraces the alphabet a few times over in her head *L,M,N,O,P...Q,R,S...A,E,I,O,U... what's going on?* She closes the phonebook and sure enough, it has this year's date on it. Why are there no Murrietas in the phonebook? How can this be?!? Josefina then thinks, *none in the hospital and none in the phonebook, what about the police records?*

"Oh wow! Did you hear that?" Alejandro says with joy as the others in the diner applaud with approval.

Josefina doesn't care about what she hears on television. Her immediate concern is why no Murrieta exists in Perilous City. *They must exist. It's a Mexican name. Surely being a large city in California someone has some variation of the name.* Even more perplexed, Josefina walks back to her plate and asks Alejandro for a to-go box.

Josefina's attention snaps back to the television screen listening to Mercedes Downey speak, "In recap, Captain Harry Love told us two members of the Peligrosa were murdered in self-defense, and three others are in the custody of the police without bail with a trial set for when they recover from their injuries. Mayor John Bigler has told us that he wants to personally congratulate this mystery person and give this hero the 'Key' to the city. Tonight, at eleven you will see my live interview with Father O'Riley on the description of this mysterious hero. This is Mercedes Downey reporting for Channel Six News at six!"

The news of her description airing at eleven tonight frightens Josefina. Would people know it was her? She doesn't want people to know. Josefina doesn't want the exposure. She doesn't want the key to the damn city. She doesn't trust the police. There is a great reason why she dislikes the police. They had done nothing for the Murrietas when they had called the authorities months before 'the incident' about harassments from the Peligrosa. Josefina heard her father and her older brother, Antonio, discuss many times how half the police force was Peligrosa. As far as she knew, there never were charges brought forth about the murder of her family. Josefina never knew the outcome of that night. She was shuffled away so fast to an orphanage and life so filled with activities, finding out why it happened was the last thing on her mind. Not now, a new interest has developed in her soul. She wants all Peligrosa to die. And she wants to be the one to do it, like they did to her family.

CHAPTER 8

# THE INTERVIEW

Tonight, Josefina decides not to venture home on foot. She flags down a taxi. What she needs is a good night's rest and a relaxing weekend to heal from her wound. But this won't be too easy. She needs to find some things out first. It is another four hours before the eleven O'clock news will come on. The entire city will be watching the report and Josefina is nervous the police could be raiding her apartment at any time. She knows if the police weren't incompetent, they would have her DNA by now. She also knows there are no records in the hospital about her or any Murrieta. The phonebook and the coroner's office have no information about Murrietas. Josefina decides to do some more detective work.

She quickly makes a list in her mind of people and entities that should have information about her. Josefina, unintentionally, has made herself unreachable; she has no phone, no cell phone, no relatives, and no close friends. She has never stepped foot into the Department of Motor Vehicles so there is no driver's license or community identification card for her. In fact, Josefina has no documents that could support who she is. Her birth certificate, social security card, and all her belongings went up in flames ten years

*A Legend Awakens*

ago. There is even a lack of work records because she "fell" into her job four years ago.

From day one at the orphanage, Josefina, took many classes at the gym. She was a presence there every day for six years. When she left the orphanage, Josefina continued her daily routine and her boss paid her weekly, off the books. She had private schooling, was well-educated, and did quite well. She was not interested in school, so she dropped out once she turned eighteen. She never had visitors. Josefina always pushed away anyone who was trying to get close to her for obvious reasons mentioned earlier.

Josefina instinctively thinks that the orphanage should have records. It must, after all, it is an orphanage. Josefina plans to make a trip to her home of six years first thing in the morning. Then there is the Perilous City Police. There must be records of her there. That's it. The DNA database in the city's police computers must have all her information.

The taxi drops Josefina off in front of her apartment complex. She pays the driver and then enters the lobby to use the phone. While she thumbs through the phonebook to call the police station, she realizes that she has never signed any rental agreement to stay at the apartment. In fact, she has never paid rent in the last four years. Not ever thinking it was weird when she left the orphanage. Josefina had a key given to her ten years ago with a note attached stating, "If you ever need a place to stay this apartment is yours."

This note, along with the address of the apartment, was left in a little box beside her hospital bed along with her precious necklace. When Josefina turned eighteen, she made the apartment her home. She gets no mail. If there is a problem, she sees the landlord and he fixes it. That can't be normal. The taxi drops her off at her apartment complex. Josefina heads directly to the phone in the lobby and calls the Perilous City police department.

A prerecorded message says to the caller, "Hello, Perilous City Dispatch, please hold." and then boring elevator music starts playing.

Josefina, with a roll of her eyes, disgustingly says, "Go figure, 'on hold', when you need the police."

After two very agonizingly long minutes on hold, a lady starts speaking with a condescending voice, "May I help you?"

Josefina startled out of a daydream says, "Umm, yes, aaa, I umm aaa."

The dispatcher rudely quips, "What is it? There are other calls on hold."

Josefina came up with the first thing she could think of, "Oh, I'm sorry. I have found a little boy. He's sad and can't find his parents. He said his name is, isss, Antonio Murrieta. Could you help locate his family for me or even give me a phone number so I can call them?"

The annoyed dispatcher utters, "This isn't an emergency. We're not going to send a squad car out there for a lost boy. We have more important things to do."

Josefina, not surprised at all with her answer replies, "I'll bring him home. I just need to know the address to take him to."

There is a pause then the lady replies, "Well fine. What did you say his name was? Anthony Morales?"

"No, Antonio Murrieta."

"Mam, there is no Murietta in the database? That is Murietta. You did spell it Mike-Uniform-Romeo-India-Echo-Tango-Alpha?"

Josefina, a bit discouraged and confused at first spells back, "No, that's M as in Maria, U as in Umbrella, R as in Rainbow, another R as in R, I as in Ice cream, E as in elephant, a T and an A."

"That's weird."

Josefina, hearing that exact phrase the night before when she was looking for her medical records, isn't reassured. "What's weird?"

*A Legend Awakens*

"There is no variation of Murrieta in our database. There must be a glitch."

*No glitch,* "Oh well, will you look at that," Josefina says changing the subject, "the young boy's mother just came in. Thank you for your help. Bye." Josefina hangs the phone up. *That's strange. I don't exist. The Murrietas don't exist. None of this makes sense.* She starts for the stairs, but before she heads to her apartment Josefina finds herself at the landlord's door. She hesitates for a few moments contemplating whether or not she wants to disturb the landlord. She finds herself lightly tapping on the door, tck, tck, tck. Josefina, impatiently waiting, taps again, but this time louder, TCK, TCK, TCK.

"I'm comin, I'm comin." Four deadbolts are heard unlocking then the door opens a little. "Oh… it's you Josefina," the landlord opens the door the rest of the way, "please come in."

"Hello sir, how are you this fine evening?" Josefina comfortably walks in following the old but hefty landlord. His comb-over flaps as he walks.

"What brings you by?"

"This may seem strange to you but I'm going to be blunt. Who pays my rent?"

"Your uncle does Josefina."

Stunned and thrown back, Josefina slouches down on the closest chair near her. Being very startled she asks with a confused countenance, "My uncle?"

"Oh yes, yes, your uncle, a very nice man indeed. He comes by once a year and pays me cash… a full year in advance. He's been doing this for, well, a good ten years now. For six years," he stops and thinks then continues, "yes, six years, it was empty. I had my wife dust and vacuum it once a month to keep it clean. Then four years ago you came."

In the same startled voice, she reaffirms her question, "My uncle?"

"Yes, your uncle."

Once again, reaffirming her question, Josefina asks, "**MY** uncle?"

The landlord now feeling a little confused, "YES, **YOUR UNCLE!** Why, is there a problem? He was here a few weeks ago. You're paid up to the end of the year."

Even more confused and with a blank stare she continues, "No, no, n-no, there's no problem. What's his name?"

"I don't know," quickly answers the landlord.

Very perturbed and quite annoyed, Josefina sits up straight and demands, "What do you mean you don't know? You rent him the entire top floor and you don't know his name!"

Not liking Josefina's tone, the landlord raises his voice as he answers, "Did I tell you, he pays me CASH… for a whole year? In times like these, that is all I need to know."

Josefina supports her face with her right hand moving her head back and forth into it. "What does he look like?"

"Mexican."

"Mexican? Ok, let's take this back ten years. A man saying he is my uncle gave you cash to hold this room vacant for me. None of that struck you as odd."

"Yes, that's right. Well, sort of you see. He said that a little girl named Josefina, his niece, would probably come by every now and then. He asked us to keep it clean. He paid extra for that. But it sat vacant for six years. The first year he decorated it with Mexican things, exercise equipment, and those gymnast bars. Me and the misses were shocked the day we saw you come out that door. You remember that day. I said to you, 'Miss, Miss, are you Josefina?' and you told me you were. There, I was satisfied. You have been a perfect tenant since. You keep the peace and never make a peep. Not to mention your uncle pays timely every year."

"What's my last name?"

"Not a clue and I don't need to know."

*A Legend Awakens*

Surprised by his callus reply, Josefina frankly asks, "How can you let someone live in your building without knowing who they are?"

"Listen Josefina, everyone in this building pays cash. I'm happy with the last names of Grant, Franklin, and Jackson. That is all I need to know. It keeps food on the table and me out of trouble."

"Can you describe my uncle for me?"

"Listen, Josefina, I like you so I'm going to be brutally truthful to you. Many people come in here saying they're an 'uncle' and their 'niece' is going to spend the night. Take that as you will, but my answer is Mexican. Now, you have to get going. I want to watch tonight's news. Enjoy your evening, Miss Josefina." He helps her up out of the chair and leads her to the door.

Josefina turns and says, "Thank you, I guess." The landlord shuts and bolts the door behind her. Clarification is what Josefina was hoping for, but confusion is all she got. She walks slowly, step by step up the stairs to her apartment.

After unlocking the door, Josefina steps inside then rests on the shut door behind her. She flips the switch to turn on the light and stares deeply into her apartment. Her eyes stop at every item in her apartment studying them very carefully. She has never paid for any of the furnishings she's looking at. Her home was all decorated for her when she got there. Josefina's entire Mexican heritage is on display everywhere. Besides Alejandro's diner, this is the only place in the city that makes her feel comfortable.

The apartment is accessorized with colorful hand-woven rugs on the floors and matching authentic Mexican tapestries adorning the walls. There is a black balladeer's sombrero hanging above the fireplace. Coiled up, like a black snake, around a lamp by the living room window is an authentic whip, possibly used for herding cattle. Never once did she move anything. Josefina loves the décor. It reminds her of her childhood home. The apartment is even furnished with its own mini-home gym.

The apartment is on the top floor, so Josefina has the tallest ceilings. The spacious living room has gymnast uneven bars. There is even a balance beam along with tumbling mats for her intense aerobic workouts. She enjoyed her fencing classes at the orphanage and was ecstatic that the apartment had a couple of fencing épée hanging in the living room. She practices with them as often as she can. But there will be no exercising tonight… she is exhausted.

Josefina prepares herself for bed. She pulls out of her backpack the first aid kit from work and tends to her arm again. To her, it looks like she did a great job. There is no sign of infection, but she is sure there will be a huge scar. She is trying her best to fight the urge to fall asleep. She too wants to hear about the Perilous City hero. It is another two hours before the eleven o'clock news. Josefina's eyes become extremely heavy, her head keeps nodding up and down while she sits on the couch gazing at the television. With one last nod of her head, Josefina falls asleep and starts to dream…

It is a late spring afternoon and Josefina looks like she does today as a twenty-two-year-old woman but she is acting eight years old. The Sun is shining bright in the cloudless blue sky this late summer afternoon. Josefina's home is how she remembers it, well maintained and the yard well-groomed with bright green grass. She is merrily playing hopscotch on the sidewalk when her brother Antonio finishes restoring his classic Indian motorcycle. The clear coat was buffed to a very high gloss giving the motorcycle a gorgeous multicolored-metallic flaked black paint shine. He calls over to his younger sister and asks, "Josefina, would you like to go for a ride?"

She stops playing instantly and runs to her brother, "Si, Antonio. Me gusto su motocicleta."

Lifting his sister off the ground and sitting her on the motorcycle, Antonio straddles the bike with her in front of him. The Indian turns over with the first kick. A rumbling thunder exhaust note can be heard down the street with every rev of the throttle. The engine is running smoothly with no skips. Antonio shifts it into first and the thrust from the launch wedges Josefina into her brother's chest with the wind blowing on her face. They ride all over the city with people pointing and smiling at the beautiful bike. Josefina feels very safe and secure on Antonio's motorcycle.

During the enjoyable ride, Antonio and Josefina arrive in a dark alley. At this point, Josefina feels very nervous. She looks all around and becomes frightened. All the walls are graffitied with Peligrosa skull markings. Suddenly she and her brother are yanked off the bike and surrounded by a score of Peligrosa. The group of villains is pushing and shoving the siblings. They are motionless and unable to move. Josefina feels completely useless. From the crowd of assailants, a familiar Peligrosa walks towards them. It's Ricardo. He approaches with his yellow-stained smile. While flicking a cigarette in their direction, he kneels in front of the two frightened Murrietas. The laughing Ricardo pulls out a gun and shoots Antonio in the leg, then in the arm, and continues until he empties all the rounds into her brother. Josefina tries to fight back but she is frozen. Ricardo jumps on the bike and drives off smiling with his missing teeth and forehead tattoo entrenched in her mind.

Josefina keeps struggling as the Peligrosa continues kicking her and Antonio. Antonio with his last breath tells his sister, "Remember the family legacy." Josefina watches as the Peligrosa drags her brother away and throws him into a large bonfire. The dread that fills Josefina's heart hurts her dearly. The pain of loss makes it impossible for Josefina to breathe and she starts fighting back tears. The swarm of Peligrosa turns back towards Josefina demanding her gold. Their hands are all over her pawing at her clothes removing gold nugget after gold nugget--

With heart racing and tears flowing down Josefina's cheeks, she startles herself out of her nightmare. She snaps her head back and screams for her brother while swinging her arms trying to grab back her nonexistent gold nuggets from nonexistent assailants. She confusedly looks around to get a grasp on her surroundings. It takes Josefina a few moments to get her thoughts realigned and her bearings straight. After several eye rubs and sitting up straight, Josefina is now more alert than she was earlier in the day. Josefina hears someone talking and finally realizes it is the television set. Father O'Riley is on the television, and he doesn't look so good.

Besides the welt across his head from the previous night, Father O'Riley looks like he was recently assaulted. She thinks, *He didn't look like that last night. In fact, I don't remember him having his arm in a sling this morning when he was waving. I wonder what happened. Did the police or the Peligrosa hurt him again? What am I saying? They are one and the same.* Josefina awoke in time to hear his description of the hero.

With teary eyes and a frightened expression Father O'Riley gives his Irish-accented description, "I didn't see much. I was previously knocked out by one of the Peligrosa," the Father pauses for some composure, "but I guess I have to give you this description."

Mercedes Downey butts in, "It will surely help the public find this hero so we can honor him properly."

In a muffled tone and looking down away from the camera as if he is ashamed to talk, Father O'Riley says, "She is a young woman."

"A woman!?!" Mercedes looks shocked. Even with her sleuthing, she had not heard it was a woman before. She, like most of Perilous City, except the Peligrosa, assumed it was a man who took out six bad guys.

Father O'Riley now with a grin and a happier tone, "Yes, a young and beautiful woman. She was an angel sent from God to save this church and this city," then he glances off stage and quickly changes back to his somber mood.

*A Legend Awakens*

Mercedes, agreeing interjects, "Yes, Father you're right… this city does need something to get its mind off the crime. We want to celebrate but we need to know who this heroic woman is."

"I don't know who she is. I've never seen her before. As I already said, I was unconscious through everything. I woke up just in time to see her leaving. She was dressed all in black. The poor lady had blood all over her face that kept her hair, her dark hair stuck in place. I couldn't see her except for the most haunting gorgeous green eyes."

The seasoned reporter interjects, "Well we now know she is a woman with green eyes. You said she had dark hair. Was it black or brown?"

"I really couldn't tell. I guess it could have been dark brown. But there was so much blood. It could have been a deep auburn red."

"How tall is she? How big is she? She must have been a very large woman to take six Peligrosa out."

"Oh, no, no, she's no taller than I am. I'm a short Irish man. The Lord himself gave me an intimidating height of five feet five inches. She had a long overcoat on, but if I had to guess her weight, I would say about a hundred pounds."

Mercedes continues questioning the father, "Really? She was that small? So, our hero's or should I say heroine's act of bravery is definitely a miraculous undertaking."

"Oh, yes, most definitely. I wish I could give more information. I just saw her as she headed out. That's all I can remember." He looks right into the camera with a deep gaze that Josefina feels is for her and ends his description with, "I'm sorry."

"You were fantastic, Father." As she thanks Father O'Riley the camera angle switches to another man. It was Mayor John Bigler. The stagehands remove the microphone from the father and lead him off stage. As he is being escorted off stage, Mercedes starts interviewing the mayor with a hint of sarcasm, "Hello Mayor Bigler. It is an honor to have you with us today."

Like a spoiled child who doesn't know any better because he has never been scolded and has always had things go his way, John says, "I know it is. But I don't want to take the importance out of this situation. Our city, the lovely Perilous City has been under attack by vermin and scoundrels for far too long. We have had a major financial burden brought upon us with tight budgets. This is why I have not taken a pay raise in two years. I personally have made sacrifices in my lifestyle and live within my 1.5 million dollar salary so you, the taxpayer, could sleep at night without worrying. Our streets are the safest they have been in many years. We have repaired all the potholes, replaced all the broken curbs with new curbs, and added more stop signs and easy access one-way streets to keep our streets safe. But this isn't a re-election year, so I don't have to brag about my steps of improvement. I am here to honor a hero. I am extending a hand, out to our new hero. Please don't be afraid. You have this city's protection. Yes, you killed a couple of people, but we understand the circumstances. There is a warrant for your arrest, but I say here in front of thousands of registered voters, I will use my powers to give you a pardon and the key to the city. We are here for you, so please be a good citizen, and turn yourself in. We will see justice prevail."

The camera view pans back to an open-mouthed Mercedes with a dumbfounded look on her face. She has completely neglected that the interview is live when she says, "Thank you, Mayor Bigler. But I'm a little confused. What you said was completely irrelevant and made no sense at all. That's not why the streets are unsafe, no one's losing sleep because you're rich, and telling a hero she is going to be arrested—"

John, completely oblivious to his stupidity childishly replies, "I don't like that tone, Ms. Downey. I'm the mayor. I will pardon her."

Mercedes tired of his stupidity sarcastically remarks, "Pardon? Please come again? I'm sorry? What did you say? Could you repeat that? Did I just hear you right? John, you're only a mayor, you can't pardon anybody. You must be governor to pardon someone."

Very irate now John snaps, "That is **MAYOR** to you and to everyone watching. I am in charge here. What I say is law!" At this point, the news broadcast goes into a commercial.

"Wow!" Josefina reaches for the remote and turns the television off. She laughs to herself. *All right, I don't have to worry about anyone looking for me. I'm sure the mayor's meltdown will be all the news tomorrow. The city doesn't care about heroes. They're too scared.* Josefina doesn't care if there is a warrant for her arrest. No one will know it is her with Father O'Riley's vague and partially inaccurate description. Her brown eyes in no way resemble the haunting green description the father gave. The description was so vague it could be anyone. With the television turned off, Josefina retires for the night to the comfort of her bed.

CHAPTER 9

# DON'T CROSS THE MAYOR

Back at Channel Six, a very upset mayor is scolding Miss Downey, "What the hell are you doing out there!?! Do you not want to work in MY city!?! Miss Downey, I will see to it personally that you won't make a single news broadcast again!" Some of the mayor's men pull him aside reminding him there are cameras present. He brushes them off and continues his tantrum. Mayor Bigler snaps again and points at the cameras as he says, "Destroy those cameras," then he points at a very scared news anchor, "and Mercedes, pack your bags. You're done! Get the hell out of my city." Mayor John Bigler stomps out of the building. His entourage, with the cameras, follows him out.

While Father O'Riley is waiting for a taxi outside of the Channel Six's News building, he watches the mayor climb into the waiting limousine yelling at the driver to take him home. Father O'Riley then notices Ricardo approaching the limo. Before the driver speeds off, the scruffy Ricardo opens the limo door where the mayor is sitting and asks, "How'd it go? Did he get the description right?" Ricardo doesn't notice Father O'Riley waiting outside of the news station. Father O'Riley hides within earshot behind a cement support beam.

*A Legend Awakens*

The arrogant mayor reassures, "Oh, I KNOW it went well. I reaffirmed why I'm the one in charge. No time to talk, my dear Ricardo, I must go. We'll have lunch sometime." As the mayor was shutting the door he remembers how he was upset with Miss Downey. He quickly reopens the door and yells to Ricardo, "Oh, that news lady, you know the one. The one who's named after a car…, Mercedes, get rid of her! Let me make it clear, I don't want to see her in my city again. I told her to move, so make sure all her personal items are gone too."

Ricardo nodding his head in happy acknowledgement asks, "Where does she live?"

"How the hell do I know? What do I pay you for? Do I have to do all the thinking? You're the thug, geez!" said the perturbed-looking mayor. "Just get it done. And do it right. Her talking back to me tonight is not good. All because of that little girl, everyone is saying this city is unsafe. That's so untrue. I need you and the rest of the Peligrosa out there keeping people scared and afraid. I don't need a revolution on my hands. Most importantly, find her and kill her." He then demands his driver, "Peter, take me home."

"That's what I do best." Ricardo shuts the door and lights a cigarette. He watches the mayor's limousine pull away and walks away while mumbling, "How the hell am I gonna find where Mercedes lives? I could place another visit to the captain. Shit, I'll just have her taken out Monday when she gets to work. I just don't know what time she gets there. I could post a couple of guys there all day…" Ricardo walks past the concrete pillar where Father O'Riley is hiding. As Ricardo walks by, the father stumbles backward, giving away his position. Ricardo looks over and sees the scared man, "Well good evening, Father O'Riley. How's that arm doing? Ha, ha, ha. I think I've been a bad boy. Please pray for my soul."

With legitimate fear, based on their last visit, the father chokingly says, "There is no help for your soul. No point in praying for you. You're already destined to live your life in eternal damnation with your Peligrosa associates."

"You're so kind, Father. Behave or I'll have to visit you again. Is that new alarm system up and working? I guess the only way to get that cross out now is to destroy the church."

Father O'Riley, very angry with Ricardo threatening the church, raises his voice, "You'll do no such thing! God will stop you!"

Ricardo turns around and saunters towards Father O'Riley and in a mock Irish accent says, "O'really, O'Riley. Yer got that much faith in yer God do yer? Yer think he can stop me. He didn't stop me with this."

Father O'Riley puzzled asks, "With what?—" CRACK!

"HA, HA, HA, HA, Ha, Ha, Ha, Ha, ha, ha, ha, ha…" Ricardo's laugh fades away as he heads towards his bike. He lights another cigarette, starts his bike, and drives off.

The religiously proud Father O'Riley is on the ground holding his newly broken nose. Mercedes and some of the Channel Six employees waited for Ricardo to leave before they came out to help him. Mercedes kindly removes the scarf she was wearing and hands it to Father O'Riley to hold with pressure on his nose, "Father, are you alright? You…," Mercedes points to an employee and orders, "Ashley, get your car! We have to get Father O'Riley to the hospital. I think his nose is broken. Father, are you all right?

"It will take more than a broken nose to keep me down. The Lord will prevail. But young lady," Father O'Riley is helped up by a couple of members of the news crew. He places his other hand which is in the sling on Mercedes' lower arm, "you have to be careful. You need to get out of this city right now!"

"What do you mean?"

"The mayor, he wants you gone."

Mercedes rolls her eyes, "Oh, that temper tantrum the mayor threw back there. Don't worry about him, he's harmless. He was just upset at what I said. The truth hurts."

*A Legend Awakens*

"No," he shakes her arm that he was holding to get eye contact and with desperate urgency, he tries to reinforce, "you don't understand! He gave the order to that menacing man on the bike. He gave the order to have you killed!"

Mercedes, backing away from Father O'Riley's grip shook her head, "That can't be."

"Yes, yes it can be. I know, I heard it. Trust me, he will do it too. This Monday… before your program, that's when it will happen."

"Don't worry about me. He won't do it. Besides, I usually get here at two, the Peligrosa will still have their hangovers."

"Please go. Save yourself!" the father pleaded.

Ashley finally arrives with the car. Father O'Riley is helped in. He lowers the window and as the car drives off, he says, "Mercedes, please believe me, he will kill you!" The car drives away with Mercedes and her cameraperson watching.

Her main cameraperson, Victoria, asks her, "Do you believe any of that?"

Shrugging off the warning, Mercedes seems unalarmed, "Don't worry about me. The entire city heard him getting upset. He isn't stupid enough to do anything."

Victoria, who is very concerned, "I don't know about that. His men took our cameras. I don't know. And seeing Ricardo with him, the rumors with his connection to the Peligrosa ain't that farfetched…"

Mercedes, seeming very confident and carefree cautiously comforts her caring cameraperson," I'll place a call to Captain Love. Don't worry though. The mayor's not that stupid."

"Yeah right, I recorded the broadcast. He sure seemed stupid to me. How he wins election after election is beyond me. Maybe you should listen to the priest and take some time off. Get out of this city."

Again, shrugging off any attempt to get her to leave, Mercedes holds her ground, "No, I won't be bullied. I want to find this heroine. She did something in this city that no one has done in over a decade. She took a stand. They want to arrest her. I can't let that happen. I have the power of the media to save her."

"Oh, come on Mercedes. That's ridiculous. She murdered two people. She should have called the cops. She broke the law."

"It's a good thing you are union, or I would get you fired for that. What she did was right, and more people need to do that."

Victoria, serious about her stance continues, "Vigilantism is an unsafe practice. At what point do you cross the line? I think MURDER is a big step over that line."

Now in a protective mode, Mercedes states, "It was self-defense!"

The two of them head back into the building as the cameraperson says, "You don't know it was self-defense. The priest admitted to not seeing anything. Once the cops got there, she split. How do you know she's not a Peligrosa and tried double-crossing them? How do you know the priest didn't do it? If you ask me, there are too many unanswered and suspicious questions left wide open."

Mercedes smirks, "You're as stupid as the mayor."

CHAPTER 10

# A New Face

It's the morning of the fifth, a new day arises... a longer day. The sweltering heat intensifies as the day progresses. It has been thirty-six hours since the Peligrosa's plan for stealing the cross was foiled. There is surely another ingredient floating in the air of Perilous City. This ingredient's source is the byproduct of Josefina's action.

Surprisingly, while her body has been healing from the bullet wound, Josefina awakens stronger than one would expect. She slept soundly without any interruptions and without any dreams like she had the night before. Josefina sits up in the bed and drops her legs to the ground. She's hoping her arm would be feeling better and it was. She raises it above her head with just a little pain. Josefina sits on the side of her bed pondering, *now what? I'm a wanted woman with no one knowing who I am. The orphanage, I have to go there today.* Josefina cleans and redresses the injury again. After finishing her leftover chili for breakfast, Josefina treks to the orphanage.

The orphanage is a couple of streets north and to the east. Josefina hasn't been there in four years. She moves rather quickly through the streets. Being a Saturday, the standard Monday through Friday nine to five employees are off the road. Sure, people are still shopping and selling, but it isn't as crowded as it would be during the week. It's late in the morning and Josefina makes her way to the building she had spent six birthdays, six Christmases, six Thanksgivings, and six instrumental years of her life. She made no attempts to have friends. She made no attempts to love anyone. But this building does give her fond memories. She was treated very well and cared for.

Josefina finds herself on the doorstep hovering her hand over the door contemplating to knock. At eye level was a Peligrosa symbol that turned Josefina's stomach. She thinks, *these skulls need to be removed.* She knocks. Josefina's edginess and impatience are getting the better of her. After several more knocks, no one comes to the door. Josefina reaches for the doorbell, so she presses it numerous times. She can hear it ringing, but that is all she can hear.

"Mam, may I help you?" an older lady asks from the sidewalk, which startles Josefina, making her jump.

"Oh, Hi! Yes, I'm trying to see if anyone is here."

"There hasn't been anyone living there in a couple of years." The older lady said while tilting her head looking a little puzzled, "Do I know you?"

"I don't think so. Why did the orphanage close?"

"This wasn't an orphanage," the old lady says with assurance.

"Oh, yes it was. I used to live here."

The old lady now getting a better look at the stranger smiles and says, "I knew you looked familiar. You were the little shy girl. I'm sorry to tell you, but no one has been here in over two years. I remember that night all too well. I live right next door you know."

Once again puzzled as if this was now becoming the norm for her, Josefina asks, "What happened?"

The old lady somberly tells her, "The Peligrosa chased your aunt away."

*A Legend Awakens*

"She wasn't my aunt. This WAS the orphanage," then pointing up towards the third-story window, "I was privately taught right up in that room. I used to look out that window."

The old lady confidently tells her, "Dear, this wasn't an orphanage. I assumed she was your aunt. She always had nieces and nephews coming and going. You were here the longest. But, I guess all that doesn't matter now with the Peligrosa chasing her out."

"What do you mean the Peligrosa chased her out? Did she move?"

"You truly don't know?"

"No, I don't. I came here hoping to get some answers and all I am is more confused. Where did she go?" The heat is now bearing its wait on Josefina. She exhaustedly asks, "Do you know where she moved?"

"No, young lady, she didn't move. They chased her out and killed her in the street. They beat her in front of everyone. The police arrived too late."

With more hatred filling her soul for the Peligrosa, Josefina stands tall and straight, grits her teeth, and under her breath hatefully says, "They always arrive too late." The lady raised her for six years and Josefina has no more tears to shed. Josefina stomps down the stairs disappointed with another dead end, zips past the old woman, and heads back into the direction of her apartment. Josefina's stride picks up to a fast pace as she passes pedestrians focusing her thoughts on what she didn't know. *Why did my family die? Why wasn't it an orphanage? I was told it was. Who is paying for my apartment? Why don't I exist anywhere? I have lived in this city my entire life. Born here, grew up here, cried, laughed, learned, and lost here...why, why, why...*

After a couple of hours of walking aimlessly, Josefina decides to go to the shopping mall. She's looking for things but doesn't know what. The mentally distracted young lady walks into an optical store, approaches a wall display, and stares at different types of glasses. Josefina now realizes she is looking for a disguise. *Since I don't exist, I might as well have some fun with it. I don't care if I live or die. I have nobody. I can fight. I can defend myself. I am very fast and agile. Being a superhero is stupid, but why can't I fight crime until I can't fight anymore?*

The optical store specialist approaches Josefina and asks, "Hello, I'm Bailee, do you need any help?"

*Why does everyone assume I need help?* Josefina's annoyance calms down when she grasps the concept that she is the customer, and the lady is actually asking if she needs assistance in purchasing glasses. *This is her job. What do I need?* "Yes, I am looking for glasses?"

Bailee still smiling asks, "For reading or everyday usage?"

"I don't need them to read. I have perfect eyesight."

Not missing a beat, Bailee continues, "So you need them for work. Like eye protection."

"No, I don't need them for protection. I don't know exactly what. Just to look different… you know hide my face."

"Why would you want to hide your face? You have such beautiful face?"

Josefina thinks, *why can't anything be simple?* "Just to look different… that's it. No reason… just to look different."

"What do you plan on doing while wearing them?"

"What does that matter?" Josefina is getting a little upset. She just wants glasses.

Bailee can tell the young lady is confused. She starts to answer her question, "Well, you see, I'm not trying to be nosy, I just want to sell you the correct pair of glasses. Let's say you plan to go out dancing. The wrong pair could keep flying off your face. They make different types of glasses for many different activities; sports, riding, goggles…"

"Wow, I didn't think it would be so tough to decide on a simple pair of glasses. I do plan on dancing and aerobics. I will be sweaty."

Very happy to get closer to her goal the optical specialist goes on, "Well then, we have narrowed the search from hundreds of choices to just a few. Here, let me show you these activewear glasses we have," she leads Josefina towards a small wall of active wear glasses. Most of them are dark glasses that Josefina likes but none are menacing. The lady continues, "Do any of these immediately interest you?"

Josefina tries on a couple, looks them over through the mirror, and says, "Yes they do. But I don't think any will work. They probably will get in the way," she then thinks to herself, *I guess the Clark Kent disguise won't do.*

Bailee brings Josefina to another area and sits her in front of a book, "Maybe something in here will give you that 'look' you're hoping for."

Josefina opens the book. It's filled with many types of vanity contact lenses. A big smile grows across her face as she flips through a couple of pages. She comes across a page of animal eyes. She finds a menacing-looking lens, "That's the one! Those will be perfect!"

"Very nice choice," said the optical specialist. "We have these in stock. Are they something you will be wearing every day?"

"I don't know. Not regularly? Why?"

"If you plan on wearing them every day, like all contact lenses, they will need to be discarded periodically." Bailee is very informative on the lifespan of the lenses and proper usage. She helps Josefina by showing her how to put them on her eyes. "How do they look?"

Josefina smiles, but not just with her mouth. She smiles with every muscle in her face, "They look great!" She blinks a few times and says, "They feel odd, but you said I will get used to them, right?"

"That's right. It won't take long. They look fantastic on you! Nice choice."

In the mirror gazing back at the both of them are two menacing electric green animal eyes.

After a couple of intense hours of shopping Josefina decides she has had enough of the mall. She waves down a taxi and returns home to her apartment. Exhaustion creeps in. Josefina is still not in top physical condition, but her exhilaration keeps her feeling a hundred times better. Josefina grapples with her bags squeezing them through the doorway before her. She places all her bags from the shopping spree on the coffee table in the living room.

Looking back and forth between the bags from her shopping spree, Josefina's excitement is overwhelming. She keeps rubbing her hands together and bounces on the couch cushion as giddy as a child on Christmas morning. Without favoritism, she starts rummaging through her bags. The first items Josefina removes from her bags are many medical supplies she figures would come in handy in the future. She places her contacts to the side, very pleased with that decision. While at the mall she purchased several body-hugging burnt orange workout outfits with matching color sweat jackets. They aren't a bright orange but a dark dull orange with a deep reddish tinge very similar to the pelt of a fox. She purchased some black running shoes and a sleeker black backpack to match the shoes.

Josefina packs some of the items she figures may come in handy inside the backpack. Only the essentials like duct tape, a flashlight, wire cutters, cosmetic mirror, razorblades, plastic zip ties, and a few other trinkets. Josefina grabs one article of each of her new wardrobes and dresses in them to see how she would look. She slings the backpack on and then brings the makeup she picked up at the cosmetic store and the contact lenses to the bathroom. Josefina pulls her hair back tight to her head and then brushes it giving herself a bushy tail behind her head. Instead of purchasing a mask that would be annoying around her face, Josefina applies non-shiny flat-black hypoallergenic makeup giving her the appearance of a mask. Now, it was time for the contacts, which Josefina struggled to put in. She stands looking in the mirror and utters, "Not bad, but it's missing something."

The makeup and new eyes disguise her face but the bright bathroom lighting shows that her disguise isn't to Josefina's liking. Then a creative idea pops into her. Josefina quickly jogs back into the living room spinning towards the fireplace. Above the mantle is a black sombrero. She takes it down and wipes some dust off it. She looked inside the hat to make sure nothing was living in it. Catching her eye, she notices some strange stitching inside the hat. Written in cursive is, 'J. Murrieta.' Josefina immediately thinks, *I don't remember this hat. This was never hanging in my home. How strange.* Josefina shrugs this odd thought off, putting it away with all the other oddities she has uncovered in the last forty-eight hours.

Josefina runs back into the bright bathroom and adorns her head with the black sombrero. Slowly raising her head, the shadow cast onto her face gives it the finishing touch she was looking for. But it was missing one thing... something of intimidation. Josefina scuttles back into the living room and grabs one of her épées from her wall sliding it through the strap of the backpack on her left side above her waist. She stands tall and proud in front of her workout mirrors hanging in her massive living room admiring her outfit while thinking of a name to call herself.

She boisterously announces, "Foxy Lady!" She stands there for a while looking puzzled, "Well... a little corny. It sounded better when Hendrix said it. It needs a little work. Now, let's see what trouble I can get into." Josefina puts on her black trench coat, which hides her épée but leaves a noticeable bump on her back where her backpack is. She checks to see if her precious metal talisman is around her neck and heads for the streets.

CHAPTER 11

# ON THE HUNT

Josefina is running on pure adrenaline from a very busy day. She's now traveling the city in her new disguise. So much for taking it easy tonight. While on her adventure, Josefina thinks, *two nights ago, I was very nervous walking these streets. Now I feel invigorated. I underestimated how hot I would be in this trench coat. It's not like I can just prowl around the city with a sword showing in public. I'll have to rethink the coat. A lot of traffic on the streets. I'm sure I stick out. I think I'll stick to the darker alleys.* The alleyways are safer when it comes to dodging bullets, but violence can be just as bad. Josefina weaves in and out of the first alleyway without any confrontations. Some of the vagrants just look up and then go back to drinking their liquid comfort. After half an hour looking for some action Josefina is in the church alley from two nights earlier.

The church lights are on. *I wonder… are the lights on for the new security or are they trying to steal the cross again. If they're trying to steal it again, then I'm sure they're guarding out front.* She tries to open the door that leads to the alley, but it's locked. Sneaking in is something Josefina is going to have to figure out if she doesn't want to get caught.

*A Legend Awakens*

The bell tower, Josefina figures, should be the best way in. She looks straight up to try to plan her ascent. It takes a few skillful minutes to scale the church to the top. Besides a little pain in her left arm, it turns out to be quite simple. Josefina looks over the edge and sees two police cars parked out front guarding the church. *I'm glad I took the alley. I'm definitely noticeable. They probably would've thought I was the lady from the other night. Even those inept police would be suspicious of me.* Josefina goes back to the bell tower to figure out how to get in. The belfry has some wire mesh in place to keep out the bats and pigeons. The wire mesh is in between spacious wooden slats. There's enough space between them, Josefina is sure she can squeeze through it. Josefina removes her trench coat and instantly feels relief. *Now, I have to get the wire cutters.* It isn't easy reaching into her bag to retrieve the cutters. She draws her épée and removes the backpack to find them. Josefina cuts the mesh out from between the two slats. Josefina pushes her bag through first then squeezes herself through with no issues leaving her épée and trench coat behind. She shuffles through her bag to pull out the flashlight.

The shine of the light reveals a stairwell just six feet from her. It doesn't take long to descend all the stone stairs while collecting years' worth of cobwebs. There's a wooden door at the end of the stairwell. It's held shut by a simple latch. The hard part is the simple latch is on the other side, and a key is needed on this side. *Damn!* Josefina runs up the stairs and retrieves her épée. She makes it back down the stairs a little more fatigued, but her épée fits perfectly in the gap to lift the latch.

Josefina is now in a little corridor that leads to the back of the church. When she enters, Josefina is directly across from the Golden Cross. Father O'Riley is patching the last of many bullet holes in the pews with wood putty. Josefina creeps from behind and startles Father O'Riley when she says, "That's one nasty bruise on your face, Father. It must have been hard to knock out that Peligrosa with your hurt arm."

The father spins around so fast and he exclaims, "It's you! Thank the Lord it's you… and you're safe. I've been praying for you since Thursday. The night God sent you to us."

Sounding very secure and confident, Josefina assures the priest that she doesn't need anybody to pray for her. She then tells the father, "Seriously Father, it's Perilous City that needs your prayers."

Father O'Riley is worried for this mysterious woman, for La Santa Maria, and for the city, "My dear child. The police are right outside. They have a warrant for your arrest. How did you get in here? I'm sorry for the interview. I was made to speak."

"Don't worry about that father. Your description was vague enough. Who hurt you? I saw you Friday morning with Captain Love and you were fine. Then I saw you on the news. Your arm was in a sling and now you have a bandage on your nose. Was it the Peligrosa again?"

Father O'Riley, being a little embarrassed and ashamed of his condition tells the brave young lady, "Don't worry about me child. The Lord is looking over me. I am concerned for you though. I don't know why you wear a disguise, but I know you must do so now. I see you changed your eyes."

"Well, yes, someone said I had green eyes. I can't let the public down."

Father O'Riley asks, "Why the animal eyes and the fox red jumpsuit?"

Josefina smiles and says, "Remember the Peligrosa you knocked out?"

"Yes, I do."

"Well, he mentioned I was as cunning as a fox. There you go… the outfit."

*A Legend Awakens*

"What you did was so wonderful the other night. I will forever be in your debt. Whatever you need; support, sanctuary, an alibi, anything at all I will be there for you."

"Thank you, Father. I may require your help someday. In the meantime, please spread the word that there is a new justice in town and that she won't rest until the streets are safe again. Try to encourage everyone to keep the faith and stand up for what's right."

Father O'Riley, remembering his encounter with Ricardo the night before urgently warns, "There is someone who needs your protection."

"Who is it, Father?"

"Mercedes Downey, the Channel Six news anchor. Do you know her?"

"Yes, I watched the fiasco last night."

"She needs your help. I heard the mayor tell Ricardo, one of the evil Peligrosa gang members, to take her out. He is going to take her out in front of the station when she arrives there this Monday. You must stop it! I don't think she believed me. She gets there for two."

"So, it does go to the top." Josefina is not surprised.

"Yes, I am afraid so. He wants you killed as well. I heard him last night. The Peligrosa are told to find you at all costs. So please, be very careful."

"I'll do what I can for as long as I can. In the meantime, Father, please tell everyone to keep their eyes peeled. I will help them as much as I can but they need to keep their eyes and ears open for me."

"What is your name, young lady?"

"You can call me... Sly Fox...," Father O'Riley looks at Josefina a little puzzled expecting to hear a proper name. Josefina notices the bewildered look on his face and continues, "I know that sounds a little randi," she chuckles then concludes, "I'm still working on a name. We'll keep in touch, I got to go Father." As quickly as she was in the church, Josefina leaves, vanishing from Father O'Riley's view, slipping unnoticed out the back door.

On her journey through Perilous City looking for Peligrosa, Josefina, adorned fully in her outfit, hears some commotion at the end of one of the alleyways. Three punks are knocking down the makeshift shacks belonging to the homeless individuals being harassed.

The tallest of the assailants is sternly saying, "We've got to find her! If any of you'z guys hear or sees anythin you'z better tells us quickly or we'll do more than knock around your piece-of-shit cardboard boxes."

Forcing as tall of a stance her body frame can muster underneath a dim streetlight with her face hidden by the shadow of her black sombrero, Josefina summons as alarming of a voice she can, "And what do you rejects plan on doing after you find her?"

The Peligrosas' heads abruptly turn in surprise. The tall one, pointing his finger in her direction, annoyed by the interruption yells to her, "Get the hell out of here if you knows what's good for ya."

A little shocked by the stupidity of the ignorance in front of her, "You are as imbecilic as the man you work for. I'm the one you want! Leave them alone. You have done enough damage to this city. If you know what's good for you, you will leave now!" Josefina's heart is racing. She eyes her surroundings to find easy escapes. There are a few garbage cans suitable as a quick source of shelter and a couple doorways she may have to dive into for cover. Other than that, she is an open target.

Two of the Peligrosa drop the people they are holding and push them onto the ground. Then the three attackers amusedly walk towards her. The smallest one (who is still quite taller and much larger than Josefina) in a very deep voice says, "This little thing roughed up the other guys. Can we have fun with this zorra

*A Legend Awakens*

first before we kill her?" He winks and kisses the air in Josefina's direction.

The tall one who is obviously in charge says, "I don't seez why not." Standing a couple yards away he looks her up and down, "I likes what I seez guys. Let's have fun!" The three headed in for the attack.

Dripping in sweat, Josefina grabs the hilt of her épée nestled on her hip and quickly pulls it out. The extremely sharp tip accidentally slices her backpack strap. She feels the weight of the backpack shift to her right shoulder. She thinks, *using a backpack strap as a scabbard ranks pretty low in the smart scale.* With one decisive swipe, Josefina did, however, successfully snag the small Peligrosa's lip ring while simultaneously sliding the épée through his ear plug. Then the three thugs thwarted their thinning thrust thinking that they had no idea what was going to happen next. A glimmer twinkles in Josefina's eye as she smiles and winks at her captive. Within a millisecond Josefina has one Peligrosa so frazzled he is moving like a marionette with every tiny wrist movement of his captor. Josefina smirks and taunts the other two, "Now gentlemen, do you want this to continue? I'll be awfully disappointed if you don't."

The middle-sized Peligrosa who is quite puzzled nervously states, "She's gots one of them dancing swords. Aren't those fake?"

Again smiling, feeling the advantage, Josefina replies, "Numbnuts, there's no rubber tip on this one and it's called an épée. Trust me, it's very real and very, very sharp!"

The tallest Peligrosa pulls out his gun and tired of the game exclaims, "Joey, I don't cares if it's fake or real! Ricardo wants her dead so dead it is!" He has his gun pointed at Josefina's head. She instantly pivots on her right leg and performs a perfect roundhouse kick to the gun-wielding assailant's lower jaw sending him spinning to the damp and scrungy pavement. Because of his irrational action, the knocked-out Peligrosa has a broken jaw and his partner is now missing half his lower lip and left ear lobe.

Josefina chuckles when saying, "Oh, I'm sorry about that… here maybe this will make you feel better." She pounces on and knocks down the one she just disfigured. After several swift punches to his jaw with the hilt of her épée he too is unconscious.

CLICK, a deep voice says, "Don't move." Joey, the third Peligrosa has his gun pointed at the back of Josefina's sombrero. Hearing the hammer of the gun go backward, Josefina ducks and turns to the right as he shoots—BANG! The bullet moves straight and fast but misses her. The bullet lodges into the disfigured Peligrosa's forehead eliminating the horrid tattoo. Joey turns around trying to find where she went.

"Over here!" Josefina yells.

The Peligrosa turns and fires—BANG! By this time the remaining residents of the dark alley are standing out on the street watching from a safe distance. He continues holding the gun with two hands in front of his body turning in circles. "Where are you?" Joey asks then jumps around and aimlessly shoots because a garbage can lid flew by him—BANG! Then a brick lands at his feet from behind. He turns—BANG! Another brick smashes the only working light in the alley—BANG! He hears Josefina giggle—BANG!—BANG!—BANG! Then the only thing that echoes through the alley is CLICK! CLICK! CLICK! CLICK! CLICK! Joey flips open his revolver and dumps the shells on the ground. He begins fumbling in his pocket for more rounds when a dark sleek figure comes up from behind.

"How sad… no more bullets… bad news for you," Josefina says while standing in a ready fighting position behind the frightened Peligrosa. Joey quickly scampers away and trips next to a doorway. He nervously struggles to his feet. With his back to the door, he suddenly cannot move anymore. The épée has pierced his right shoulder sticking him to the door. "Now listen and listen well,"

Josefina is on her toes gazing deep into the eyes of this Peligrosa while wiggling her saber. With every twist more pain comes to Joey's twitching face and the bigger Josefina smile becomes. Nodding with her head back to the left she tells Joey, "Your friend there is unconscious so you'll have to relay this message. This is the last time I will let any of you walk out of this city on your own. This terrorism must stop. You tell Ricardo I will be coming for a visit."

Staring gauntly into this young fearless lady's haunting green animal eyes keeps Joey mesmerized. This Peligrosa's breathing becomes very intense. He warns Josefina with an interrupted out-of-breath slur, "You gotz no clue what you got yourself into! The Peligrosa works for money. We aint yur only enemy. This entire city is corrupt. You got a long hard road ahead. You'll be dead, zorra." Joey spits in her face because he is beaten and there is nothing else he is able to do.

Josefina, not liking the slang 'zorra' annotation, knees him hard and fast in the groin. She pulls out her épée from his bloody shoulder. He falls to his knees. Josefina bends down and with the tip of the épée, she makes several quick motions disfiguring his Peligrosa tattoo. She takes his gun and puts it in her bag. Josefina runs over to the Peligrosa that she knocked out, and with another three fluid motions with her épée, she disfigures his Peligrosa tattoo as well. She grabs his gun then goes over to the dead Peligrosa and stands above him. Josefina smiles at the bullet hole replacing his tattoo. The crowd from behind starts cheering at the spectacle they just witnessed. Josefina waves to them and says, "People of Perilous City, a new dawn has risen. The 'FOX' is here to bring justice back to the streets." With a disappointed thought, *I got to work on that, how corny.* Josefina disappears into the night.

CHAPTER 12

# A Bounty On Her Head

"...Three more of my men! Who is she, Wonder Woman!?" Mayor Bigler is quite outraged. He is a spectacle pacing back and forth in his penthouse office throwing his trinkets everywhere. Two other individuals are with him tonight. Ricardo, his main muscle who is leaning up against a wall, and Captain Harry Love, sitting in a chair on the other side of the room avoiding the gold knick-knacks, are eyeing each other with contempt. After several deep breaths to calm down, John says, "Has the press got a hold of this yet?"

Pocketing a few more trinkets in view of the captain but without the mayor seeing, Ricardo leaning suave-like up against a wall answers, "No, not that we know of," then with a smile towards Captain Love continues, "our friends at the police station removed the evidence. The other two are recuperating."

The mayor sternly pointing towards the captain asks, "So, who is she?"

Captain Love is very unhappy to be in the same room as Ricardo. He knows Ricardo is below his status level. Harry hates the presence of Ricardo at this meeting and despises the mayor

*A Legend Awakens*

relying so heavily upon Ricardo's help. "We don't know who she is John."

"That's MAYOR to you Captain! Haven't we had this conversation before?"

Ricardo then adds, "Mayor, I have the word out, and everyone is told to report to us."

Mayor Bigler, rolling his eyes at Ricardo, "Now Ricardo, you just told me the people in the alley were cheering this vigilante on. What makes you think they will tell you anything? Have your men get more aggressive. What about the news lady? Did you get rid of her yet?"

"Not yet sir."

"Why not? Didn't I tell you to take care of her the other night?"

Ricardo replies while puffing on a cigarette between each sentence. "Yes, you did. And we will. We're going to do it on Monday. Right before the broadcast so that the police who aren't in your pocket won't catch on to anything too soon."

"Forgive me for not trusting you. That description you beat out of the priest couldn't have been any vaguer."

Ricardo, a very pompous man, is proud of his job when he affirms, "It appears the description I beat out of that priest was accurate. Joey said her eyes were a very haunting green."

"Joey... oh yes, Joey. Isn't he the one you said could wrestle an alligator? What did she do to him? Well, as long as the alligator didn't have a sword in her hand...get out of this room and bring her to me, if not dead, very wounded."

"Yes, sir!" Ricardo leaves the mayor's penthouse office mumbling.

"Now Captain, what about the DNA database?"

Captain Love rolls his eyes while waving away the puff of smoke Ricardo blew in his face as he left. He confidently answers, "No matches in the database. I had the hospital and our department check, nothing matched. I've sent a sample to a friend of mine at the Federal Bureau to see if there is a match in their system. I should hear back soon."

The distraught mayor says, "I told you that DNA thing wouldn't work."

"John, the DNA mapping of the citizens was your first undertaking as mayor. If there are no results, it's because they are not a citizen here or by chance, the records have been erased."

The mayor stops and thinks a little bit and then mumbles, "Erasing could have occurred I guess," then in his normal tone continues, "but that's all history now. There's got to be something that can lead us to this girl. And, Captain, that's MAYOR."

"Yeah, well, there is something… something of quite an urgent matter. It appears your slacky, Ricardo, is a bigger idiot than you think. Mercedes Downey called me at the station stating something you would find most intriguing."

Waving his hand down, the mayor retorts, "Captain Love, you worry yourself too much. Didn't you just hear Ricardo? She will be taken care of."

"Not so fast John, she told me that Father O'Riley told her that you gave the order for Ricardo to have her killed."

Mimicking what the captain just said with his hand like a puppet the mayor childishly states, "I heard that Ethan told Ryan that Alex told Cole… Bah! Again, you worry too much. It will be taken care of. And that's, 'MAYOR', Captain!"

"You're missing the point. Mercedes wanting protection may cause an inquiry. Let's hope she only told me. If Mercedes told anyone else outside the Perilous City police, you may have a larger issue. She's not leaving the city and she does get a ton of viewers. And let's not forget your interview on Friday night. I'm sure your polls dropped quite a bit."

The mayor, disgusted by any talk about losing votes with a stern stature states, "They vote for me because they're afraid to vote any other way. I own this city and in another three years, I'll own

*A Legend Awakens*

California. My ancestor of the same name used to be the governor of this beautiful state. His gold was stolen from him by a bunch of low life bandits. I've recovered most of it. The largest piece I'm missing is standing securely in that godforsaken church. And, Captain, I WILL get it back. I can't believe they got a donation for a security system and with your men guarding the church until it's in place… don't you think that'll make it a little hard to steal? The only way I think will make it possible to take is to destroy the church. Besides, that church was built by HIS followers," the mayor gestures towards a dim corner of his penthouse office.

"This is foolish John. I know your family history oh so well. The gold comes from many families, not just yours. But that doesn't matter right now. Whatever vengeance you have with him is ludicrous. You have won. You're wealthy beyond all means. Besides, you can't destroy a church. If anybody finds out you're the cause of it, your insane plan of governing California will be lost."

Mayor Bigler interrupts, "That's MAYOR, Captain, and soon-to-be governor."

Disgusted with the mayor's stupidity, Captain Love shrugs off his idiotic notion. "John, can I leave now?"

"CAPTAIN Love! CAPTAIN Love! Do you see how easy that is?" John heads back to his desk sitting down on the front facing the captain then calmly continues, "Why must you show disrespect? I've earned it, call me MAYOR."

"Well, if that's all you got, I would like to finish my weekend relaxing. I'm sure Ricardo will keep me busy on Monday. Will you do that? Let me go home and enjoy a Sunday."

"Sure, you can do that, but one thing before you go. Come here," the mayor sits up from the desk and waves Captain Love to follow him towards a darkened corner where there stands a large wooden cabinet festooned with gold. Mayor Bigler opens the cabinet. It is very dark inside and appears to be empty.

"I can't see anything." said Harry. Mayor Bigler flips a switch and the internal lights shine brightly. Inside this cabinet is one item. Harry Love jumps back startled and yells, "What the!?! WHO THE HELL IS THAT?!?"

Very proud, with his hands in his pockets and repeatedly rocking up and down on his tiptoes, John boastfully exclaims, "This is my prized possession! That, my dear Captain, is no other than that head of my ancestor's mortal enemy, Joaquin Murrieta!"

The captain, now intrigued, curiously says, "THE Joaquin Murrieta," he approaches closer to look and calmly studies it for a bit. The mayor is smiling and is super excited waiting for the captain. Harry continues, "THE 'Robin Hood of El Dorado.' You mean to tell me this is the man the legendary Zorro was based on?"

Shaking his head up and down in agreement with every nickname the captain mentioned, eyes wide open, and a grin from ear to ear the mayor blurts out, "Yes, yes, and yes the one and only! You impress me, Captain. You know your history very well."

"You're telling me this head is close to two-hundred years old!" Harry walks over to the closest chair and sits down in amazement. "You never cease to amaze me, John. I don't believe it. How in hell did you get your hands on that?"

Very excitedly like a young child showing off a rock collection, the mayor, ignoring he was just called by his first name only, explains, "This is a piece of history that was lost to the world back in the great San Francisco earthquake of 1906. You see… it disappeared. Everyone was told it was destroyed. Many years ago, I was watching a show about people's morbid and bizarre collections. I saw in the background on the shelf a glass container surrounded by tarnished bars. As you can see now those bars are pure gold. All you could see on television was the back of the head. I did some research and visited this man to look at his collection. I asked him if he knew whose head that was. The man had no clue. I asked him how he came across it. He told me his great-great-great-great uncle or something like that, had stolen it from a building after an earthquake about a century ago. The story matched, so I offered him ten-thousand dollars on the spot for it. He took the offer. That is when my plan began."

Skeptical, Harry asks, "How do you know it's his head?"

"Modern science my good captain," the mayor taps the captain on his head, "modern science! I had a lab run the DNA with the hair sample and a piece of skin behind the ear. I then compared it to the DNA of known descendants of Joaquin Murrieta. It took them a while, then the results came in… EUREKA it matched!"

"Is this why you wanted the city resident's DNA samples?" The captain went into a very deep thought. He is a bright individual and seems sincere at times. That sincerity is overshadowed by his corruptness.

"Precisely," the mayor exclaimed!

Harry gazing intently into the jar holding Joaquin Murrieta's decapitated head asks John, "Do you still have those results?"

"Yes, somewhere on my desk. Why?"

"I would like to see them."

Mayor Bigler wobbles to his desk and opens one of the drawers. He pulls out a manila folder and hands it to Harry. "You will see that these are quite accurate."

The captain opens the folder, flips through the sheets, and notices many side-by-side comparisons of Joaquin's DNA samples with that of Perilous City residents' DNA samples. "So, you know all of his descendants?" While the mayor turns around and walks towards the cabinet Captain Love slides one of the sheets out and places it in his blazer pocket.

Annoyed at what was just asked, the mayor waves his hand passing on the thought, and says, "Never mind about that. My point in showing you this is that HE," Mayor Bigler points directly at the head of Joaquin Murrieta, "was the thorn in the side of my great-great-great-great-great-great grandfather Governor John Bigler!"

Mayor Bigler is pointing straight up in the air with conviction, "Now I have a thorn in my side! I would like her head to be sitting next to his!"

Harry Love, still in awe of the head asks, "You want me to bring her head to you?" Harry stands up and hands John the manila folder.

John snatches the folder and puts it back on his desk. "Of course, Captain!" The mayor went back to the cabinet and gazed into the glass container holding it on each side, "Don't you see? My great-great—"

Harry interrupts, "Yeah, I get it, go on… your great grandfather."

"Well, yes, anyways, he created the California State Rangers led by your ancestor of the same name. He, Captain Harry Love, was ordered to hunt down Joaquin Murrieta. So, you see its destiny." The mayor changes from a big boisterous voice to a simpleminded childlike voice, "He was his arch enemy, and she is mine."

"John, I'm not going to bring you her head. That is very morbid. You need help."

Pouting like a child the mayor asks, "Why can't you call me mayor? I promoted you to captain. You would think you would respect me for doing that."

As arrogant of a tone he could muster the captain quips, "I didn't vote for you."

"Oh, you're such a kidder. So have her head here as soon as possible. I don't want the people to revolt."

"The people won't revolt. You have them too scared."

The mayor brings the conversation back to his point forgetting Harry's haughtiness, "I will have a jar made to accommodate her head. Bring it here as soon as you can."

Captain Love figures this could go on all night. He decides to agree to the challenge set before him. He is tired and wants to rest before Monday morning gets here. The captain gets up from the chair near the cupboard and heads for the door. Once he arrives at the exit he states, "I do believe my ancestor got a reward when he brought the governor Joaquin's head. I expect something similar to that… Oh, because of inflation I would like it in today's values. Goodnight, John." Captain Love shuts the office door and departs from the penthouse.

CHAPTER 13

# TROUBLE AT LA TIENDA

On the east side of town, hundreds of feet below the penthouses, Josefina, who is curled up on the couch in her outfit from the night before, is waking up to a new morning. She stretches out with a large yawn. Her left arm is still sore which makes her think; *I got to get those stitches out.* Josefina heads to the bathroom and scrubs the makeup off her face. She washes the wound very well and pours some rubbing alcohol on it. It stings a little. She knows the wound hasn't completely closed, but she also doesn't want it to heal with the dental floss sutures in her arm. Josefina decides to take the chance that the wound has healed enough to adhere Band-Aids to it. She grabs the tweezers and starts pulling on the sutures. A couple of tugs on each prove to be successful. Josefina applies some antiseptic cream and then finishes dressing the scar with a couple of butterflies and an ace bandage. No doubt there is going to be a nice mark, but she feels confident there will be no infection.

Josefina finishes getting herself dressed in her normal exercise attire and goes to the uneven bars to see how well her arm will hold up. After a few swings, she realizes she made a big mistake removing the stitches. Josefina went back to the bathroom and removed the bandage. Sure enough, from the twisting on the bars, she ripped it open again. The disappointment sets in because she doesn't want to go to the hospital to get it taken care of. *What to do? There's got to be something.* Josefina thinks while looking around the bathroom and continues; *stitches won't work because I don't want it to heal with them in me. What can I do to seal this thing so I can still use this arm?* Josefina looks around her house for something to use.

She rummages through her 'utility' drawer in the kitchen where she finds some superglue. *Why not...* she thought, *it adheres to my fingers very well.* Josefina pinches her lower arm between the wall and her hip to close the gap. She cleans it again with more rubbing alcohol then dabs it dry with a towel. After a few more minutes she has it sealed tight with the superglue. For extra-added measure, Josefina cuts a sock and slides her arm through it. She then wraps some duct tape just to maintain pressure. She waited several minutes to make sure she didn't put it on too tightly. A little hesitant, Josefina mounts the uneven bars again and flips through a five-minute routine with a little bit of pain but nothing rips.

While Josefina is going through her Sunday routine of exercise and solo fencing practice, she keeps thinking about how much her life has changed since Thursday night. A couple of questions keep popping up but figuring out the answers is going to be tough. The first obvious one is trying to find out what happened to her family and the second is finding a way to continue her double life. Josefina's stomach starts growling. A quick trip to the kitchen turns up an almost empty refrigerator and a few snacks left in the cupboards. Josefina decides instead of going to the store across the road, she will go to the large market, La Tienda. She grabs her backpack with the crudely fixed strap and heads uptown.

La Tienda is on the northside of Perilous City located at the railyard which runs parallel to the San Joaquin River. It's the perfect spot for a fresh food market. It is located near one of the oldest railroad stations that are scattered throughout California. As the food comes off the trains, the vendors set up to make their quick cash. Many residents will go to La Tienda to get fresh meats, fruits, and vegetables. It's the only time these inhabitants ever come close to leaving the city and has become a regular occurrence for over one hundred years. They look forward to going because it's at the edge of the city where it is cooler with less smog. A large section is dedicated to parking spaces but instead of cars, they are mostly filled with vendors. Most people attending take the bus to get there. The restaurant owners show up in vans to take a large selection of fresh foods back to their establishments.

As Josefina's first excursion to La Tienda progresses, the humid air and vacant streets bring forth a familiar feeling of hopelessness to Perilous City. Sure, Josefina is now more confident and feels she can bring change to the city, but there is an underlying sensation crossing her mind making her feel it will be a rough road ahead. A loud hustle and bustle can be heard. The outside air temperature dropped several degrees. Josefina knows she is almost there.

When Josefina turns the last corner on the street leading to La Tienda, the marketplace opens into a vast community of its own. She is quite amazed by the large gathering. Josefina squints her eyes wishing she had purchased a pair of sunglasses. Spending her life in Perilous City under a continuous cloud of smog did have the advantage of protecting the eyes. The Sun is much brighter and more intense, but the temperature is easily ten degrees lower at the edge of town. It is very noisy but in a good community sense. Instead of drive-by-shootings, busy city traffic with obscene shouts, and heated pedestrian arguments, everyone seems to get along. There is plenty of dickering between the consumers and the vendors. The smells are fantastic. Besides just selling the products that are brought in for sale, the vendors also cook and prepare the foods to capture the customer's attention.

Several vendors sell the Sunday morning newspaper. Everyone seems to be very interested in the article on the front page. Next to a trashcan is a copy of the paper. Josefina quickly grabs the copy and stuffs it in her backpack.

The continuous aromas with the entire presentation of all the foods remind Josefina of her continuously growing hunger. While walking up and down the rows, Josefina snacks on samples. She has purchased several fruits and vegetables so she will have something for dinner tonight. La Tienda is very intimidating for a first-time visitor. For the last three hours, the young hero has been snacking, shopping, and enjoying all the art that goes into making specialty dishes. Josefina manages only to make it through half the vendors. She decides since it's midway through the afternoon, it's now time to return to her dark side of the city. She must be at work the next morning and is undecided whether she will venture out tonight. This decision is easily made when Josefina sees some movement in what appears to be an abandoned building.

At first, Josefina shrugs it off thinking the movement could be some homeless people. But her curiosity is piqued so she decides to go investigate. The Sun is now going down quickly like it always does this time of year. As she heads towards the abandoned building, she notices the crowd thinning out and the vendors are starting to pick up their belongings. Within a couple of hours, it will be dark. Deciding to go into stealth mode, Josefina creeps towards the building. The only part of her disguise she has is her damaged backpack with its contents. Josefina makes it to the back of the building to find an easier way in. The backside is a loading dock adjacent to the train tracks. There are several Peligrosa gang members hanging around on the dock. Josefina overhears them talking about a shipment that will be arriving later tonight. Josefina thinks *apparently the market isn't at its busiest on Sunday afternoons. The activities at night in this railyard should be under suspicion.* The young vigilante decides she will hang around to see what this shipment will be.

Josefina makes her way onto the loading dock and hides behind some dirty barrels that appear to have been untouched for many years. Darkness is quickly approaching. The security lights turn on illuminating most of the dock. The wait is going to be quite a while. She takes the newspaper out of her backpack and rests it on her lap. While snacking on some fruit and vegetables, Josefina starts reading the paper. The headline catches her off guard. On the front page is an article about Perilous City's new liberator:

**Back alley bullying thwarted.**

*By: Rea Peterman*

*A hero returns and, Zorra, is her name. When questioned, the residents of the alley were ecstatic finding out the legendary hero had returned in female form to clean the city from evil. Although no bodies were found, it was told Zorra left a mark defacing the Peligrosa tattoo. This brave vigilante who came to the rescue of some of Perilous City's citizens last night is believed to be the same woman who stopped the church robbery the other evening. The police aren't releasing much information. Captain Love has been unable to be reached for any comments. Continued on A-3*

Josefina whispers, "Page one again." Then she thinks, *Zorra, huh? Cute... not sure how I feel about it. Zorra is slang for tramp. For years I've never thought of it as anything else. I've started a mission to clean this city and bring it back to its original glory. Why not reclaim the word 'zorra' as well?* She spends the next half-hour reading more of the article about her. She learns that several alleyways were vandalized last night and many of the

*A Legend Awakens*

homeless people were beaten. This angers Josefina more than ever. These innocent individuals are getting hurt because the Peligrosa are looking for her.

Snacking on the perishables attracts the interest of some scavenging rats. Josefina spends some of the time swatting them away. The long wait is bothering Josefina. She is cramped in her hiding spot and since the sun is long gone, she is getting a little chilly. Contorting her body into a more comfortable position has proven to be difficult but not impossible. She will take the discomfort because Josefina's locale is ideal thanks to the barrels she is hiding behind. They are also in a spot where no security lights are directly on her. Josefina has a very good advantage point being able to see up and down the dock with no interference. It gives her plenty of time to see how massive this abandoned train station dock and warehouse actually are. Every now and then a Peligrosa traverses up and down the dock doing a lazy security check. Over the last six hours, Josefina managed to unintentionally sneak in several catnaps. She is awoken from her last one when she finally hears a faint rumbling in the background.

The loud noise of a motorcycle litters the air. It's a noise that is all too familiar to Josefina. She slides her head up from her hiding spot still concealed very well with the night. Sure enough, coming around the corner closer to her is an Indian motorcycle. Ricardo is in the saddle and rides up the ramp onto the dock. His headlight cascades along the side of the building quickly illuminating Josefina's location. She sinks back rather fast behind the barrels praying that she was not seen. Sure enough, even though her face was quite visible, no one was looking in that direction. Ricardo stops the bike about twenty feet past Josefina right in front of a shipping door.

A few of the Peligrosa who are making their rounds greet their tall-shaven boss. Ricardo continues his chain smoking when he tells them, "Alright... it should be here any moment." No sooner did he finish uttering those words, from a distance two headlights shined brightly down a side road running parallel to the train tracks. "Here it is guys! Keep your guns at the ready."

Josefina, with intrigue, peeks through the space between the barrels but the bike is blocking her view. The only way for her to see anything is to raise her head up again. Josefina carefully picks up her head and sees an armored Wells Fargo van pulling up to the dock. Josefina, a little puzzled, she thinks, *I assumed it was going to be a train.* The shipping door of the warehouse rattles and begins opening. Within seconds a score of Peligrosa is on the loading dock. Half of whom have their normal Smith and Wesson 7-shot revolvers drawn and the others are empty-handed. Heart thumping and breathing heavily, Josefina thinks *I can't dodge that many bullets at one time.* The Wells Fargo van comes to a complete stop.

Ricardo looks at his men, flips a cigarette back towards the barrels, and as he lights another cigarette says, "You guys know what to do." The driver climbs out of the armored van. Ricardo jumps down to meet with the driver. He is followed suit by three of the Peligrosa as they go to the back of the van and commence to unload it. Josefina watches them pull two hundred boxes out of the van. Within fifteen minutes the van is unloaded and all the boxes are inside the warehouse. Three Peligrosa are all that remain outside the building after the main shipping door closes. Ricardo pulls himself back onto the dock. He turns and tells the driver, "You let Mr. Serpente know that he will be completely satisfied with the product."

The driver, quite demanding with his retort, "He better be. You got what you wanted. And for your sake, it better be ready this Wednesday. If the product isn't delivered on time by next Monday, he will send his little army to visit you and your boys."

"Don't you threaten me or my guys you piece of crap! I'm not afraid of no one! You just make sure you're back here with a truck at one in the morning sharp this Wednesday. The trailer will be

*A Legend Awakens*

filled. Everything will be ready. Then it's up to your driver if it will make it to New York by Monday." Ricardo flips off the driver and heads into the warehouse. Returning the same finger gesture, the driver drives off in the empty armored van.

It's quite late and Josefina remembers that she has to save Mercedes Downey before the Peligrosa kills her. She now knows besides helping Mercedes tomorrow, she needs to come back here Tuesday night, well Wednesday morning before one. Josefina peers over the barrels and realizes that her brother's Indian motorcycle is just twenty feet in front of her. It would be risky since her disguise isn't with her, but she knows there is no better time than now to take it back.

There are three Peligrosa on the dock. With her recent past experiences, she knows taking them out won't be hard. One of them heads to the edge of the dock to urinate. The other two are talking about recent events causing their gang to shrink. Josefina takes a screwdriver out of her backpack and slyly heads for the urinating Peligrosa who is closest to her.

Within seconds, Josefina is on top of the Peligrosa. With a swift blow, the screwdriver is in his jugular. With one hand holding his mouth, she pulls him back and sets him down on the dock so he won't fall and make a noise. Josefina finishes him off by pulling out the screwdriver and slicing his forehead disfiguring the Peligrosa tattoo. She grabs his gun and places it behind her back snug in her pant waistband. Without any plan or thought of action, Josefina just acts with an uncanny instinct, turns and rushes towards the motorcycle, and quickly straddles the seat. Once she is on, she realizes she has no clue how to start it. At this point, she is no longer in the shadows and is sitting awkwardly on the motorcycle with a floodlight shining right on her. One of the henchmen speaks, "Well, well, well… this must be Zorra. You don't look like much." Josefina looks up and the two remaining Peligrosa have their guns inches from her face.

She calmly says, "That's exactly what your brethren said the night before." With a smirk, she then asks, "How did that turn out?" In her right hand, the bloody screwdriver handle is wrapped with her white knuckles. Within a millisecond the Peligrosa on her right drops his gun and is grasping at his throat with a look of shock on his face. Blood is squirting everywhere. By the time the other Peligrosa realizes that his friend has a gaping hole in his throat, Josefina leaps off the bike and already pins him face down with his gun sliding on the platform. Josefina, with a knuckle-cracking tight grip, holds the screwdriver to his temple. A big chunk of throat is dangling in front of his face. She now politely asks him, "Could you please tell me how to start the bike? I will think about sparing your life if you do."

As he watches his partner bleed out on the dock, the third Peligrosa nervously points towards the foot pedal and very cowardly says, "You need to push hard on that to start it. Twist the throttle up there to give it gas." He was pointing to the handle then he continued pointing down towards the pedal again, "You then step down on that to shift up and pull up to shift down." Then with a whimper, he asks, "Can I go now?"

Josefina smiles and says, "I spared your life for a few moments. Goodbye." She holds his head to the platform making him kiss the wood as she shoves the screwdriver through his skull. Once he stops twitching, she rolls him over to disfigure his tattoo and then does the same disfiguration to the other one. Josefina scrambles to her full backpack. She removes food to make room for the three guns. She then pushes the heavy bike to the ramp and rolls it down. Josefina pushes it for another hundred yards then after a few failed attempts she finally starts it and drives off… quite sloppily.

CHAPTER 14

# Connect The Dots

A boisterous rumbling is echoing through the streets of Perilous City. It has taken Josefina less time than one would expect to become somewhat accustomed to controlling a motorcycle for the first time. The Indian is quite heavy. She's been very cautious and rolls through the stops for fear of dumping it over. At every streetlight and every corner, Josefina checks her shoulder to see if the Peligrosa are following her. She is so careful not to topple the bike. Just ten minutes earlier, Josefina was shivering behind some barrels, and now with her adrenaline pumping, and with the mugginess of stank air, she is sweaty and blood-covered. To Josefina, Perilous City is appearing different tonight. Especially when riding on the motorcycle that she is sure was taken from her brother ten years earlier.

While riding through the city on the same motorcycle where the residents are in fear of the one who has been tormenting them for years, Josefina knows she is sticking out like a sore thumb. She must hide the bike, but thinking of a place where she can safely stash it without causing an inquisition is becoming quite difficult for her. Even though her apartment has individual garages for some of the tenants she can't take it there. Her landlord would know for sure it's Ricardo's and he wouldn't want any trouble from the Peligrosa. Taking it to the church is out of the question. The police are stationed outside for a few more nights to keep a false appearance of security. One other place comes to mind. It has a secluded alley with a dumpster. She ends up at her favorite Mexican diner, Alejandro's.

The obnoxious roaring of the Indian motorcycle entering the alley awakens Alejandro. He reaches over to his nightstand and turns on the lamp instantly blinding him. Alejandro's bedroom is just as festively decorated as his restaurant. The noise from below disappears as he gets out of his bed and limps to the window. He throws open his curtain to look down into the alley. Parked behind his dumpster, Alejandro notices a motorcycle. Instantly recognizing the black motorcycle, Alejandro out of character says, "Hijo de puta, Ricardo. I told him to never step foot on my property or… ugh, god dammit." Alejandro hobbles quickly to his nightstand and opens the drawer. He takes his revolver and heads to the bedroom door.

He removes the night robe from behind the door and puts it on sliding the revolver into the front right pocket. Alejandro flips the hallway light on and limps to the main door mumbling, "I'm going to beat him senseless." He takes the steel bat that's resting near the door. Alejandro unlocks the door then turns the lights on in the stairwell and hastily goes downstairs to the kitchen. Once Alejandro makes it to the kitchen he can hear an aggressive tapping on the restaurant's door. The streetlight casts a large shadow portraying a large silhouette of someone outside his restaurant. He approaches the fogged-up door with great hatred.

Outside the building, Josefina is trying to see into the dark restaurant. She keeps tapping nonstop trying to awaken Alejandro. As she is peering into the glass door her constant breathing is fogging it up, making it difficult to see in. She hears Alejandro unlocking the door. Josefina turns around towards the street to

*A Legend Awakens*

make sure no Peligrosa is around. She turns back just in time to duck out of the way of an incoming bat while Alejandro yells, "I told you to—PING!" The bat hits the ground with such force the sound echoes throughout the street and startles some cats in the alleyways.

Josefina, in a defensive posture, plants her feet and raises her arms. She holds Alejandro's arm back preventing him from taking another swing with his bat and urgently barks, "It's me! It's me, Josefina! I didn't mean to startle you!"

Alejandro, still quite shaken looks her deep into the eyes and says, "Oh, it's you bonita. I'm so sorry. Come in. Come in." Alejandro abruptly yanks on her arm pulling her inside. He then looks up and down the street searching for Ricardo. "These streets aren't safe at night. What are you doing out so late?" He picks up his bat again and keeps looking back and forth.

Josefina turns expecting Alejandro to be right behind her, and notices he is still in the doorway looking back and forth. She asks, "Are you expecting someone?"

Puzzled and shaking his head, Alejandro steps back into the diner and turns the many locks to the door, pulls, and pushes the handle several times until he is satisfied the door is locked. "No, well... I thought I was." Still confused Alejandro checked the door one more time and no one was there. He motions to the kitchen and says, "Come let's go upstairs." He leads her to his domicile. Josefina makes it to the top of the stairs easier than her handicapped friend. Alejandro's limp is very noticeable going up.

"You have some quick reflexes. Not too many people can move that fast...," Alejandro opens his living room door extending his arm, and continues, "please, make yourself at home." Alejandro shuts the door behind them and quickly heads to his bedroom. "Please, sit down; I just have to check on something." Alejandro goes to his bedroom window and still sees the motorcycle behind the dumpster. A puzzled look comes to his face when he mutters to himself, "that has to be his bike." While Alejandro is trying to figure out where Ricardo is, Josefina's trying to explain why she's there. All her talking is falling on deaf ears, and it sounds like mumbling background noise to him.

As Alejandro walks into the living room he hears Josefina say, "I didn't know where to go."

With a voice of concern, Alejandro finally notices Josefina's blood-stained clothing and face, "¿Estás bien? Is that blood?" He wobbles over to her like a concerned father rushing to console his daughter who just fell off a bike while learning to ride.

"Estoy bien." Josefina wipes her sweaty face and looks at the blood on her hand and on her clothes. She completely forgot about the blood squirting from the jugular of the Peligrosa she had gorged thirty minutes earlier. While looking at the blood she mutters, "Not again."

"Are you sure? That looks like blood to me. Are you in trouble?"

Josefina, shaking her head looks a little bewildered then answers back, "I just told you what happened."

"Oh, Lo siento, I wasn't paying attention. I was wondering who's motorcycle is behind my dumpster. Let me get you a towel." Alejandro heads to the hallway closet and retrieves a couple of towels for her.

Josefina speaks louder so Alejandro can hear her, "As I just said, I brought the bike here. I didn't know where to go."

With a sigh of relief but still as confused as he was when he was startled awake, Alejandro quietly says, "Good, I thought it was Ricardo's."

After he enters the living room, Alejandro hands the towels over to Josefina and suggests she clean up. Josefina takes Alejandro's advice and heads to the bathroom. Alejandro grabs a plastic garbage bag for her to gather the soiled clothing. After a quick well-needed cleaning, Josefina comes out towel-wrapped. Alejandro takes the plastic bag and then heads to his laundry room.

After he starts the wash, Alejandro opens the clothes dryer where he pulls out a clean pair of wrinkled sweatpants and shirt. He hobbles back to Josefina and says, "These may be a little big for you, but at least they're clean."

"Thank you. Alejandro." Josefina very happily took the sweats and went back to the bathroom to put them on. When she gets back to the living room Alejandro sets out some crackers and cheese and puts some water on to boil for tea. He then has Josefina sit down to relax.

Alejandro pours Josefina some tea then sits down beside her and pats her knee. "Alright, Josefina, you have my complete attention. Please tell me what happened."

All the pressure from the new things she has learned or in some cases has not learned, finally reached its limit. Josefina wants and needs to tell somebody about her entire quest from the last few days. Telling Alejandro everything is what Josefina deems necessary. She spends the next hour chaotically telling Alejandro about her adventures with saving Father O'Riley, the gunshot to her arm, and her new nighttime adventures. Josefina also went into detail about how she doesn't exist in any public records and how the residents of her city are now calling her, Zorra.

As if listening is his expertise, Alejandro's set of ears are wide open and his mouth is shut for a full sixty minutes. There are several moments of silence after Josefina finishes telling her story. Alejandro absorbed everything she said like a dry sponge soaking up water. Alejandro cracks a smile and then intently says, "Wow, so it finally comes full circle. So, you got your brother's bike back."

Josefina is a bit confused at Alejandro's response. Based on all the things she just told him. And his first concern is the Indian motorcycle, "I can't be positive that it's his bike. But I do have an odd feeling about it."

Alejandro nods his head and assures her, "Your instincts are correct bonita. That's your brother's Indian."

Adding more confusion to her adventures, Josefina asks, "How do you know it's his? Did you know my brother?"

Alejandro's mood becomes a little somber and says, "I didn't personally know him, but I was a first responder."

Ever more perplexed Josefina asks, "First responder... to what?"

"I was one of the ones who first responded to your home so many years ago. That very dreadful night..." Alejandro leans forward, grabs Josefina's hands, and looks her straight into her eyes, "I guess you're ready for it now. Based on the last few days you have grown tenfold, and you should know the truth."

Josefina has the occasional nightmare about her past and her family perishing but that is what most of her memories are... locked in dreams. She dreamt just recently about her family and her home burning down but she has been all confused with those memories and then Alejandro mentioning a dreadful night from years ago she inquires, "I'm ready for what now?"

"Well, dear, now it's my turn. You need to listen. You seem confused and need the dots connected. I have a long story to tell you." Josefina lets out a large yawn and leans onto the couch to get herself comfy for what she is about to hear. Alejandro ponders for a bit about where he wants to begin his story then starts, "Ten years ago... yes, ten years... I was finishing my rounds when I heard a call on my radio. There was a fire called in to 911 and every available unit was supposed to respond. When I got there the firemen were spraying the adjacent homes with water to keep them from burning. It was too late for your house."

Josefina stops him, "You said you were a first responder. I didn't know you were a fireman."

"I wasn't a fireman. Now, don't be upset because I know how you feel about law enforcement, but I used to be a deputy for the county." Josefina abruptly sat up and Alejandro put forth his hands in a comforting motion pulsating them back and forth, "I worked for the county, not the city. I was just outside city limits when the call came in. The county deputies are some of the finest individuals I have worked with. Your issue is with the city policía. And I don't blame you. Now, please listen to what I have to tell you." Josefina leans back into her comfortable position as Alejandro continues his story.

Alejandro is just minutes into telling Josefina about how he found her and when he visited her at the hospital when he notices she is soundly sleeping. Alejandro grabs a blanket from his bedroom and drapes it over her. He then quietly says while brushing some hair out of her face, "I guess, bonita, you are not ready for it now."

Back at the railyard, right before Josefina was attacking the three Peligrosa on the dock, the shipment arrived and was brought into the warehouse with extreme diligence. The door shuts behind the men who follow Ricardo into the warehouse leaving three unaware Peligrosa to keep watch on the warehouse's train platform. Their warehouse is well-lit inside with a lot of activity. At the far end are a dozen or so stolen vehicles that now belong to the Peligrosa. There is a lot of security inside the warehouse where it appears Ricardo's men are making and distributing illegal substances. Half the warehouse is used as a domicile for the Peligrosa where several, men and women, are lounging around high and drunk.

Inside the warehouse, Ricardo is inspecting the shipment that came in. He is talking to some of his goons, "Don't forget to be on your toes tomorrow. I need you to pick up Mercedes. I don't know when she'll get there, so, stay sober and get there early. Grab her, and have her take you to her place. The mayor wants her and her stuff gone. Use the van." Ricardo pointed to the moving van that was being used a few nights earlier at the church.

The main henchman he was talking to asks Ricardo, "Will the two of us be enough?"

Ricardo looks perturbed at his question and answers, "Of course. It's a simple grab-n-go. You've done this hundreds of times."

The worried henchman asks, "What if the fox lady is there?"

"Don't be a dipshit you dumbass!" Ricardo was visibly irritated by his question. "She only comes out at night because she's a coward that hides in the shadows. There's a good bounty on her head. If she does show up bring her too. Now get lost. I want Mercedes and her place incinerated tomorrow. I want to see that on the six o'clock news!"

The Peligrosa, still a little worried, says as he and the other Peligrosa ordered to kill Mercedes head towards the door to the train platform, "Yes, Ricardo. Will do."

Ricardo lights up another cigarette, saunters towards another Peligrosa, and orders, "Make sure Mr. Serpente's heroin is ready. That trailer…," Ricardo points to a forty-foot trailer, "needs to be ready to move out of here Wednesday at one in the morning, sharp."

This Peligrosa said, "No problem boss we are ahead of schedule. We'll be able to start the next batch shortly after. Everything is going smoothly here."

Ricardo, pleased with his answer confidently says, "Good, I don't need Mr. Serpente sending his men here."

Then the Peligrosa asked, "If you don't mind me asking Ricardo, why isn't the mayor handling Mr. Serpente?"

Ricardo with a great grin, "The mayor doesn't need to know everything that's going on in this city. With him out of the picture and the money we've made on this production, it'll now put us in a financial situation so that we won't always have to depend on his money. It'll be nice of us to have more options and more business contacts."

Just then the two Peligrosa who headed to the platform yelled into the warehouse, "Ricardo, you're going to want to see this!"

Ricardo and a few others exit the building and stand on the platform with jaws dropped. Ricardo's cigarette fell out of his mouth when he exclaimed, "What the hell happened here!?" At this point, he notices the foreheads of the victims lying on the blood-soaked platform, "That zorra! That zorra was here." He then points at a few of the Peligrosa out there with guns drawn, "Do a perimeter search. Close the station down. She's got to still be here. We were all out here no more than twenty minutes ago!"

The Peligrosa, who were ordered to kill Mercedes, points to the spot where Ricardo's motorcycle is usually parked and then with extreme concern asks Ricardo, "Do you still think the two of us will be enough if she shows up?"

Totally ignoring what was just asked of him and not caring about the dead people he just walked by, Ricardo with arms wide out gesturing to the empty spot where his bike was twenty minutes earlier yelled, "That zorra took my bike. Forget the mayor wanting her head. I want her and I want her alive! That stupid zorra! Who is she? Where is she? I want everyone looking for my bike!" He then looks at everyone standing still. Ricardo grabs his revolver, aims it in the air, and fires a couple of rounds. The Peligrosa start scrambling while some wood debris from the overhang above rains down on Ricardo's head and shoulders. Ricardo looks down and sees a few vegetables lying on the platform. He then kicks at them sending them flying into the dark.

CHAPTER 15

# Zorra To The Rescue

With eyes shut tightly, Josefina's intense slumber comes to an end as an amazing aroma of Mexican food fills her nose stimulating her olfactory senses. She gives out a large yawn and stretches her body long and hard pulling the blanket off her. Josefina glances around to get a grasp on where she is. After realizing she is still in Alejandro's apartment, Josefina calmly calls out, "Alejandro!" With no answer back she rises off the couch holding the bulky sweatpants up to her waist. On the coffee table next to the couch are her clothes from the night before all washed and folded.

It's eleven in the morning, the beginning of lunchtime down in the diner, and Alejandro is busy hustling in the kitchen with the preparation of his customers' lunches. Josefina comes down the stairs and sees more people in the diner than she has ever seen before. She quickly throws on an apron and starts helping Alejandro bussing tables and taking orders. Two steady hours go by with preparing to-go and dine-in orders. Josefina answers one of the calls and the customer asks if the lunch order could be ready in fifteen minutes because they would arrive at one-thirty to pick it up. Josefina quickly hands the order to Alejandro and says, "Sorry Alejandro, I've got to go. I have to be somewhere real soon."

*A Legend Awakens*

"¿Qué pasa? If it's the gym, don't you worry about it, I already told them you were here helping me. They've got you covered."

Josefina whispers to Alejandro so none of the patrons would hear her, "I have to get home to change to save Mercedes Downey."

Alejandro suggests, "Maybe we should call la policía." No sooner did the words leave his lips, Alejandro realized he shouldn't have. "Lo sé, lo sé…I know, go back upstairs. When you fell asleep, I took the liberty to gather some of your things from your apartment. What you need is up there in the bedroom."

Josefina asked puzzlingly, "Wait? What?"

Alejandro with a big grin reinforces what he had just said, "Up in the bedroom, I took the liberty of bringing your outfit here."

Josefina, extremely worried about how much time she has left to save Mercedes, heads upstairs to Alejandro's bedroom. Amazing, her entire outfit is strung out on the bed with a couple of new accessories. Josefina, without hesitation and without questioning how her disguise arrived, puts her contacts in, dons her apparel, and applies the makeup to her face all under ten minutes. She ties her hair up into the bushy foxtail. The additional items there are two belt gun holsters, two ankle gun holsters, four handguns, and a bullet-proof vest. Not being ungrateful, but Josefina remembers what bad aim she had a few days back in her confrontation at the church. She leaves the guns behind. The bulletproof vest is too heavy, so she leaves that on the bed as well. She does, however, utilize the other item that is left there: a proper sheath for her épée. Fully disguised, Josefina pauses in front of a mirror and with a smirk says, "Hello Zorra." She then looks herself up and down and asks herself, "Did you leave the trench coat at the church?"

Zorra darts for the stairs, halfway down she remembers she doesn't want people to see her running through the diner. She turns around immediately and darts back to the bedroom. She runs to the window and halts when she notices security bars. With a quick study, she realizes they do not appear to be too close together. Zorra

105

ponders, *if my head can fit the rest will follow*. She opens the window and with a little force her head fits through. She then brings her arms through and pulls herself out onto the window's ledge. She is just on the second story so the jump down to the dumpster doesn't look too menacing for her. There is a bit of moisture in the air, which could make the condensation on what she thinks is the dumpster's metal lids a little tricky. Zorra quietly whispers, "Here goes nothing." She turns with her back towards the bars and ungracefully she takes the leap. BANG! THUD!

The metal lid turned out to be a very slippery hard plastic lid and Zorra slid off the lid as quickly as she hit it. "Ouch, that was stupid," Zorra scolds herself. She had landed on the lid with her feet which quickly turned to her sliding down the lid and then flipping to her back on the ground in front of the dumpster. Zorra sits up and is now soaked sitting in a puddle. She has no time to worry about that now. She must get moving fast to the Channel Six News' news station. Zorra scuttles behind the dumpster to where she left the motorcycle. *Great,* she thinks, *every Peligrosa will be looking for this. Not to mention they will hear it coming a mile away. I have to get there fast, and this is the only way to do it*. Zorra starts it up after a couple of faulty tries and notices the motorcycle is no longer as loud as it was before. *Apparently, Alejandro changed the muffler on it. He got my clothes. I wish I didn't fall asleep last night.*

Meanwhile, a couple of miles away from the diner and across the street from the Channel Six News' news station, two Peligrosa are impatiently waiting inside a black van waiting for Mercedes Downey to start her day. At about 1:45 in the afternoon, a taxi pulls up and Mercedes climbs out. She looks around and sees the black van across the road. She scrambles through her purse looking for money to pay the cab driver. Mercedes gets really nervous and fumbles a bit at her wallet.

"That's her," anxiously yells the Peligrosa in the passenger seat while pointing excitedly at Mercedes, "quick let's get her!"

The driver announces, "Hold on!" as he puts the van in drive and depresses the accelerator.

When the van's wheels start squealing, Mercedes hands the cab driver more than enough money and frighteningly says, "Keep the change," then she quickly turns and heads for the building.

The taxi driver who is used to dropping her off says, "Thanks Miss Downey, don't you want your receipt?" He watches her as she keeps briskly walking to the building.

About ten yards before the entrance, the Peligrosa's van drives on the crosswalk, cutting off traffic and almost running over several pedestrians. The van jumps the curb and comes to a screeching stop right in front of Miss Downey. Mercedes lets out a very loud scream as the van door slides open.

"You're coming with us," said a Peligrosa as he yanked her in.

Mercedes keeps screaming, "HHHHEEEELLLLPPPP!!!!!" but to no avail. As quickly as they stopped, she is hoisted inside the van, and they were peeling out.

As the van squeals around the corner, Zorra shows up from the other direction on the motorcycle through the clammy mist that has descended onto the city. Zorra slows the motorcycle down and notices the confusion from the bystanders and the stopped traffic from the Peligrosa zooming out of there. The cab driver shouts out, "Zorra is that you!?"

Still frazzled with the difficult ride getting there, controlling a motorcycle too big for her and in pain from her descent onto the ground, Zorra answers back, "Yes, what happened?"

The cab driver points in the direction they took Mercedes, "That way! The Peligrosa took her! Hurry they just left!"

Zorra sees the wet tracks turning the corner then speeds up and heads in pursuit almost losing control of the motorcycle. As she drives off, the witnesses applaud and take pictures.

Inside the van, Mercedes is giving the thug who grabbed her a hard time by kicking, screaming, and twisting. The driver barks at his partner, "Get control of the situation! We've got a job to do!" The one struggling in the back takes out his gun and shoots Mercedes in her right leg, the same leg that had just nailed him in his crotch. BANG! The shot echoes in the van momentarily deafening the assailants and the victim. The gunshot did its job… Mercedes is now motionless.

With muffled hearing, the Peligrosa who shot her shouts, "Where you live?" Mercedes, grabbing at her leg and seeing the blood coming out, faints.

The driver then yells back at him with ringing in his ears, "You dumbass, now how are we going to find out where she lives?"

"I don't know," the Peligrosa in the back stupidly says as he shrugs his shoulder.

"You better put something on that leg so she doesn't bleed out. We need to find out."

The Peligrosa takes some rags and wraps her leg with it. While he is lifting her leg, Mercedes awakens and nervously asks, "I suppose you're going to kill me?"

The driver says to her, "The mayor wants you to leave the city, so we are going to your place and get your things and take you out of this city. So, tell us where you live so we can get this done."

Mercedes shakes her head refusing to tell them. She knows that the mayor wants her gone and they will probably make it look like she moved.

"Do you want me to shoot her again? I know, wait a minute…," finally being smart he then grabs her purse and rummages through it taking out her identification card, "…there." He hands the driver her driver's license.

The driver studies the address on the card. Her ID has her old address from when she worked in a small town about sixty miles south of the city. The Peligrosa then says, "You live there? That's a hell of a commute." He heads towards the highway taking them out of the city through the southbound lane of the tunnel. Mercedes

*A Legend Awakens*

starts crying uncontrollably, wishing that she had listened to Father O'Riley.

The assailant in the back stands up with a large dirty grin swaying as the van moves and says, "Since we have her address, I guess we don't need her alive. She's such a pretty lady. I'm going to have some fun with her before I waste her. You know, give her one last moment of pleasure."

His friend in front, while glancing out his driver's side mirror, says, "You know, I wouldn't normally mind, but I suggest you tie her up and get up here. We have company. We don't want her dead yet."

The Peligrosa in the back grabs a roll of duct tape and starts taping Mercedes' legs and arms then puts a piece over her mouth. He crawls into the front passenger seat and looks out his mirror. He sees a small rider on a large bike and says, "Is that her?"

"It sure is. It gotta be. She's been following us for about three miles now. That's Ricardo's bike. I know it." He grabs the cell phone from the dash and calls Ricardo. "Hey Ricardo, we've got Mercedes."

Ricardo answers back, "Good, good. Something's finally going right. So, I take it everything is going smoothly. Did you find out where she lives?"

"Yeah, I got that right here. But I have even better news for you."

"What's that?"

"Your bike, and that zorra is following us. Where would you like me to bring her?"

Ricardo angrily and excitedly yells into the phone, "She's on my bike! Continue as planned. This time she can't get the jump on us. Once you get to Mercedes' place use her as a hostage so Zorra gives up. If you have to, shoot her, but don't kill her. I want her alive. You have the upper hand. Let me know the moment you got her."

"Will do boss."

Zorra, although very frightened to be on the motorcycle, is finding it easier to ride. Tailing the van is easier than she thought. *Why aren't they speeding? They have to know I'm behind them. They're leading me to a trap. I have to stop this on my terms.* Zorra speeds up and rides parallel to the van right in front of the sliding door.

The Peligrosa from the passenger seat tells the driver, "She's pulling up. Why don't you run her off? We're coming up to the tunnel. She's going to hit the wall if she doesn't back off. I think she's going to try to climb on."

Annoyed, the driver begrudgingly answers, "Ricardo wants her alive. She's not going to climb on dip-shit. This ain't the movies." No sooner did those words leave his mouth than the van door slid open. The driver turns his head and sees Zorra grabbing the side of the van door and leaping inside the van. The moment she climbs into the cargo bay of the van the motorcycle wobbles out of control and hits the back end of the van then veers right into the guardrail where it then ends up smashing into the entrance wall of the tunnel.

Zorra quickly assesses the situation. Although she is limited toward the back of the van, Zorra sees a glimmer of hope in Mercedes' eyes. When she turns her attention back to the front, the Peligrosa has his gun drawn and facing her. He then says, "So you're the Zorra chick? You don't look like much. You're a tiny little thing." He then tells the driver, "Keep driving, I got this under control." He keeps his gun with the hammer drawn back pointing it directly at Zorra and nervously says, "Now I'm gonna shut this door… you stay back." As he leans for the door the outside air blows his hair and Zorra sees the haunting Peligrosa tattoo on his forehead. Again, all rationale disappears. And why not… within the last half hour she jumped out of a second-story building and leaped off a moving motorcycle at forty miles per hour. Zorra pivots on her right foot and with her already sore left leg she lets her hips lead the way to a perfect roundhouse kick. She knocks the off-balanced hoodlum in the head sending him flying out the door

*A Legend Awakens*

directly to the road where the tunnel traffic behind finishes off the Peligrosa.

"Oh shit!" the driver exclaims. Within milliseconds of her kick, Zorra pulls out her épée and performs a limpy balestra ignoring her pain. The tip is now pushing on the driver's carotid artery. He, still thinking he has the upper hand says, "Listen here zorra. I've got my seatbelt on, so I suggest you put the sword down or I'll slam the brakes."

Zorra gleefully smiles at him through the rearview mirror and while trying to muster a little, "Inspector Callahan," she gives a scowl then deepens her voice and says, "Go ahead punk, make my day. The forward inertia will slice your artery right open. You're gonna have to ask yourself one thing, 'Do I feel lucky?' Well, do ya? You'll bleed to death while I'll be thrown forward a bit. I wouldn't slam those brakes… unless you feel lucky punk. I suggest you look to see where my other arm is." She sees him look in the mirror again and he now notices her left arm tangled in a cargo net that is braced to the wall of the moving van. Then she tells him, "Go ahead reach for your gun. You'll bleed out before you get a shot off at me. The only way you'll get out of this van alive is if you stop it nicely. So, what will it be?"

The Peligrosa says to her, "You zorra. We've done nothing to you. Why are you doing this to us?"

"You have done plenty to me and my city. I'm just cleaning up the trash. Now are you going to be a smart Peligrosa and stop this van nicely?"

"You promise you won't kill me?"

"I told you I will let you out of this van alive. You have no other choice now do you?"

The Peligrosa gives a wicked smile and confrontationally adds, "You think you're so smart, zorra! I got news for you. I do have another option." He then shifts the van down a gear and depresses the accelerator pedal to the floor. The instant rise in RPM tosses

Zorra backwards releasing the épée from his neck. He then slams the brakes as hard as he can and sharply turns the steering wheel to the left sending all the loose items from the back of the van towards the front ejecting most of the loose objects, including Mercedes, out of the side door. Her body hits the pavement rolling several yards up the tunnel. Because of this impulsive action several cars initially collided with the van then a domino effect of southbound traffic came to a disastrous halt causing a massive pile-up.

The squealing of the brakes, metal-on-metal crashes, and explosions from all the collisions echo through the tunnel. After several rolls, the van is upside down and slightly spinning. After the van stops spinning Zorra untangles her dislocated arm from the cargo net and then falls to the roof. She crawls to the front of the van where the Peligrosa is hanging upside down. She looks dumbfounded when she says to him, "What were you thinking?"

He then nervously replies, "Help me! Please, help me!"

One of the cars that crashed into them knocked the engine loose and it had pushed the steering column into his chest. Zorra looks at him and says, "I'm not a doctor, but it looks like you will be dead soon enough. I don't think an ambulance will make it to you in time. The pile-up is too severe." She grabs a piece of glass and disfigures the tattoo on his forehead.

"I can't feel my legs. Help me! Don't leave me here…" his yells are useless… Zorra has no emotions of pity for any Peligrosa.

Zorra climbs out of the wreckage and hobbles over to Mercedes. On the way to her, she picks up her épée and puts it back into her sheath. Zorra frees Mercedes from the tape. Besides bumps and bruises and a gunshot wound to the leg, she is relatively unscathed. Zorra's left arm is dangling low. She asks Mercedes to pop her shoulder back into place. At first, Mercedes doesn't want to because she doesn't feel comfortable doing it. Zorra says, "Please, I need to see if I can save anyone in that pile-up." Mercedes reluctantly does it and after a couple of attempts sure enough it pops back into its socket. Zorra feels instant relief.

Zorra stumbles towards the wreckage when a couple of explosions occur. She is thrown to the ground. The heat and smoke are too much and start bringing back horrible emotions from her childhood. She freezes and can't go any further. While Zorra is watching the fire engulf vehicle after vehicle a hand grabs her. Mercedes says, "Zorra, we have to go, if we stay any longer the smoke will kill us." Mercedes helps Zorra to her feet and together they limp out of the tunnel.

After their quarter-mile walk to the end of the tunnel, they are finally in fresh air. The intense brightness catches them off guard. The smoke is billowing out of the tunnel and a few more explosions can be heard. Distant fire truck sirens are audible.

Zorra snaps out of her daze and anxiously tells Mercedes while tugging on her, "We got to go!"

Mercedes trying to not budge and needing medical assistance for her leg says, "We can't go. We need medical attention."

With urgency, Zorra tries reasoning with Mercedes, "You don't understand. I can't be found. The mayor wants me and you dead. And now he thinks we are. We need to go into hiding. Come on. Let's go. We can't go back through the tunnel, so we'll have to hike around or go over the mountain."

Mercedes, standing her ground says, "I can't do that. I'm not like you. I need to get help. Thank you for saving me. You go. I won't tell anyone you survived. I'll tell them you went back in to save the rest and never came out."

The sirens are getting closer so with no more time for further pleading or arguing Zorra leaps the embankment and starts climbing the mountain to head back to the city.

CHAPTER 16

# NEVER ENDING NIGHT

When one is wearing the wrong footwear the mountain's rocky terrain makes for difficult footing. Sneakers may be good on cement, but every step is an arduous one with Zorra's foot slipping out causing loose debris to cascade. Zorra looks down as she climbs to see the commotion she left behind. At this vantage point, being that she is halfway to the top of her vertical assent, she can take a break without worrying about being seen. She finds a spot for herself to rest. With no skyscrapers and no smog, it's very bright on this side of the mountain. Zorra's dark burnt orange outfit blends perfectly with the colors of the rocks she is climbing. Although there is a plume of black smoke pouring out of the tunnel her visibility to the chaos below is unobstructed.

At this time, the Channel Six News, the police, and the fire department's helicopters are circling the exit of the tunnel. Zorra counts twenty emergency vehicles that have finally arrived from surrounding communities. The city has shut off the northbound entrance so that they can get the emergency vehicles through. Traffic can be seen blocked for miles. Zorra feels horrible. There is no telling how many innocent lives perished today because of her reckless behavior. *I caused this,* she thought to herself, *what was*

*I thinking? This is my fault.* The dread of this afternoon's accident started weighing on her. She cries uncontrollably into her hands.

It takes quite some time for Zorra to gain her composure. She wipes away the tears and turns to finish her mountainous climb. With the drastic increase in altitude, the temperature drops considerably fast. By the time she reaches the pinnacle, the Sun has disappeared from the winter sky. Not used to the temperature drop, she is shivering. Now she is back on Perilous City's side of the mountain, which is a sheer rock cliff with no light for her to see. To descend at night is going to be impossible and to survive without freezing would be equally impossible. The wind is whipping very hard. The canyon walls would most definitely be a death trap. Zorra thought back to her schooling and then remembered where she was and what those mountains were used for two hundred years prior.

"Think Josefina, think," Zorra starts mumbling to herself while shivering, "We were a mining town. These mountains must have a means to get down. The tunnels below were used as forty-niner tunnels." Zorra is walking along the ridge of the mountain. On the north side below is her city covered in smog and easily thirty degrees warmer. The brightness of the city above the smog is quite charming... at this perspective. She finally sees how high some of the skyscrapers are. So high they are above the smog. And she can see Mayor Bigler's penthouse. She says with anger, "The rich even breathe better than us." Then she notices something very unusual. The way the wind is blowing she can make out swirls moving on the top of the smog only to be dispersed in the center of the city by Mayor Bigler's skyscraper. She says with her teeth chattering, "That horrid building is preventing the smog from draining away."

While not knowing what to look for and searching for anything, the shivering Zorra sees something amazing that she has never seen before, a full moon and a sky full of stars, "Wow, how gorgeous!" Off in the short distance, Zorra sees a light shimmer on the ground. She heads towards it and sparkling on the ground is a reflection of light from the moon. It is reflecting off a stainless-steel handle from an access port. Zorra gets down on her knees and starts to sweep away the dirt from this, four feet square opening and sadly notices it's locked. The hinge that's connected to the latch appears to be the thinnest part, therefore, the weakest section. Zorra picks up a rock with her frigid hands and starts smacking the hinge. After several hits she notices the hinge becoming deformed. After twenty minutes of constant banging, with different rocks, the hinge breaks free.

Zorra struggles a bit to open the lid and she gives it one final push and it flops hard on the ground. The full Moon shines enough for her to see down for at least a few dozen feet. This is what she is looking for… an abandoned wood-planked elevator shaft. At this point staring down this dark hole, she asks then answers, "Why didn't I take my flashlight? Oh yeah, it was daytime. I hope those old wooden planks hold me." Zorra sits on the edge. She places a foot on one of the side beams giving a lot of pressure, it bends a bit, "Here goes nothing." She stands up and puts her entire weight on it. It arches even more but doesn't break. She starts descending carefully, being very cautious with every creaking step. And with every step, she clears more and more cobwebs.

As Zorra's descent progresses, the Moon moves in a more favorable position shining up the dark shaft. It is much warmer and without the wind, her mood improves. She needs her energy to make it down safely. Looking up, she can see by the dwindling size of the opening she has climbed down a very long way. Her arms and legs are exhausted. Let's face it, she has recently abused her body with very little time to heal. She knows she must keep moving… no time to rest. With the bright full moon directly above, Zorra takes advantage of the moonlight lighting the way she looks down. Way off in the distance through the cobwebs, she can see some more shimmering. Zorra loosens a piece of wood and drops it. She counts, "One Mississippi, two Mississippi, three Mississippi…," she watches the wood crash through the webs finally causing a rippling below. The moment she reached "six Mississippi" was when the wood finished its fall.

Zorra again recalls her schooling, "Standard temperature and pressure, 'STP', a free-falling object falls at 9.8 meters per second squared. It took six Mississippis, so six squared is thirty-six Mississipis. Thirty-six times ten is three-hundred-sixty. I'm about three-hundred-sixty meters above which appears to be water. Times that by three... I've got around a thousand feet to go. I think that calculation is about right." She then looks up and down again, "That's assuming the cobweb didn't slow down the wood. It's awfully thick. It's a long way. I'm also assuming that is sea level down there. Who knows how deep it is?" Zorra contemplates if she should head back up or continue down. The pain in her arms and legs gives her the answer. She continues down. Every step is a cautious one because she doesn't want to break a board and freefall down the shaft into the unknown.

While she is climbing down Zorra keeps mumbling to herself, mostly arguing and double-guessing what she has done. For the last couple of hundred feet, the raunchy smell of stagnant water was getting stronger and stronger. The smell is atrocious at best. Zorra arrives on her last dry step in complete darkness. The size of the opening above is gone from sight. Zorra's eyes are irritated with her contacts and are fully dilated trying to take in any form of light to no avail. Her own breathing echoes. The steep climb down, hand-over-hand, foot-over-foot took its toll on her fingers. Mountain climbing is not what she is used to, let alone a vertical descent on wood planks. She lowers her hand down to the rung near her knee getting a good grip before lowering her right leg. Sure enough, her foot gets wet. With dread, she lowers her other leg. She is waist-high in the most putrid of smells, but she is on solid rock. The odor is rancid, and she cannot see.

Zorra takes a step and slides on the slippery algae below her feet and instantly becomes submerged. Every time she pushes up with her feet she keeps slipping back in. All the walls below the water line are covered in algae so getting a firm grip is difficult. She reaches above the water line to grab the wall. After several attempts, she is back to her feet spitting. While spitting and wiping her face with her hands Zorra thinks, *Uggh, how nasty.* She vomits a couple of times and then dry heaves. Zorra very cautiously holds onto the wooden planks running horizontally in the shaft. She makes it to one of the walls feeling a metal bar at about chest high, beyond that is nothing. She whispers, "This must be the elevator's safety gate." In complete darkness, Zorra climbs over the old elevator rail and is now in an old miner's tunnel.

The tunnel that Zorra is now in is just as slippery as the bottom of the elevator shaft. She finds it easier to move floating in the water with her legs up and pulling herself along the planks. Holding her breath only tires her out so she tries to ignore the stench. Every now and then she gets a splinter. The ones sticking out she removes with her teeth the others, well she just has to hang tough. After thirty or so minutes her butt and legs finally hit something. The floor is now just covered in inches of water. Zorra knows the tunnel is ascending. Within another slippery dozen yards, she is now walking on a dry solid floor. She whispers, "Thank goodness."

Still blind as a bat without echolocation, Zorra walks cautiously holding her épée in her right hand in front of her wiping down cobwebs and her left fingers brushing along the wall making sure she is going straight. She knows from a few side steps and getting down on her knees that she is following old tracks that the minecarts and possibly the miners rode on. Just lifting her hand, she can feel the mountain above her. The mine can't be more than six feet tall. After what feels like an eternity Zorra's épée jabs something. She has finally reached the end of the mine. She's hoping she has reached the way out. After a few knocks Zorra realizes that they are wood planks. Still in complete darkness, she winds up as much power as she can muster in her right leg and launches a strong front kick on the boards in front of her.

Resonating through the mine is a loud, "OW!" Zorra yells in pain not knowing if the boards moved, but by the sharp twinge in her ankle, she knows it didn't. She starts feeling the wall. She can feel wood planks and within the spaces, she can feel dirt, not rock. Zorra's fingers are just too worn out to dig with. She takes her épée and rests the bulk of it on her right shoulder while she holds the tip and starts scraping at the dirt. About five minutes into borrowing a small hole the épée slips through. She pulls it back and a bright beam of light shines through. Zorra quickly peeks out of it and the brightness instantly blinds her. After several hours in the dark, she must give her eyes a chance to adjust.

Zorra is working in a small inch space between the planks trying to dig the hole larger. With every push of her épée more and more light shines through. The sun is low in the sky and a rush of very fresh air comes through. Zorra keeps kicking the board several more times to loosen it from the solid dirt. Ignoring all leg pains, the more she kicks the more she hears the dirt from behind fall. After a good hour of digging, kicking, and tugging she finally pries the plank loose. Using the recently freed board as a battering ram, Zorra repeatedly smacks the dirt wall until it crumbles leaving a large gaping hole. She clumsily climbs through and falls to the ground.

Lying on her back looking up into the gorgeous blue sky, Zorra has no clue where the tunnel has led her. For sure she knows she is not on the city side of the mountain. Being trapped in a dark and quiet tunnel for the night brings the joy of sight and noise when she sits up with her back against the abandoned mine's blocked entrance. The morning sun is warming her face and it feels wonderful. Zorra looks at her hands... they are covered in dirt and blood. The blisters, splinters, and bruises are unsightly. Smelling her sweatshirt's sleeve, Zorra is disgusted, "gross, I need a bath and a manicure." She shut her eyes soaking in the sun. Within seconds she falls asleep.

Zorra awakens hearing vehicles passing by. She struggles to her feet using the blockaded entrance as support and with painfully sore legs she heads towards the direction of the vehicle sounds. She comes up to a metal fence which in normal circumstances would be an easy obstacle. Now, it might as well be the Great Wall of China and she scales it with difficulty. She finds herself staring at the northbound entrance of the tunnel that leads into the city. "You got to be kidding me… all that work and I am on the other side of the road. There is no way I can't make it up that mountain again. Going around will be just as exhausting." Zorra whimpers at the thought of how much time and effort she wasted. Over the wall that separates both tunnels, she can see smoke still emitting from the southbound exit.

The southbound tunnel's four lanes of traffic are still closed so the northbound tunnel is being used for both directions. The traffic has slowed down quite a bit. She notices in the distance a couple of car carriers coming. "That will do." She slides down the embankment and as the second car carrier comes by, she uses the last bit of adrenaline, runs along the side of it, and climbs aboard. Zorra shuffles to the front of the carrier and sits with her back to the truck's cab as it enters the city. She is sitting on a trailer full of new sedans. One of the dealerships is up the street from Alejandro's. To get there, the car hauler will be passing her street. She waits for the proper time. As the truck slows down to make its turn, Zorra tucks and rolls and scoots into her alleyway. After she excruciatingly climbs the fire escape, Zorra disappears into her apartment.

CHAPTER 17

# A Day Of Rest And Learning

Zorra enters her apartment through the fire escape window which she has learned to keep unlocked when she heads out since her first time using it last Thursday. She scuttles to the laundry room, painstakingly takes off her clothes, and throws them in the washer. She makes it to the bathroom. The reflection in the mirror is an indescribable filthy mess. One can't distinguish the difference between the dirt and muck from the smeared black make-up mask. The dirt and cobwebs from her tunnel escapade make her hair look unrecognizable. She scrubs her fingers clean and painstakingly pulls out the splinters that she couldn't pull out with her teeth. The feeling of relief when she takes out her contacts is euphoric to her eyes. Josefina looks in the mirror and says, "You look just as you feel." After a long and relaxing aromatic bath, Josefina goes to the kitchen and devours the remaining leftovers she has in her fridge and crackers from the cupboards, then crashes into her bed for a long-needed slumber.

There is no tossing and turning. Just like the previous day when Josefina fell asleep on Alejandro's couch, she awakens to an amazing aroma of food. Josefina lets out a great yawn and stretches until every joint in her body pops, "Oh that smells good" she says while holding back another yawn. Suddenly, with a panic alertness, Josefina's eyes are abruptly open. She jumps off the bed remembering she is in her own apartment and has never smelled anything like this coming out of her kitchen before. There is someone in the kitchen. She can hear the clank of pots and somebody humming. Josefina murmurs, "that humming sounds familiar." Josefina cautiously leaves her room and heads towards the dining area. To her surprise, Alejandro is in the kitchen making dinner.

Alejandro turns around to see Josefina and a huge smile comes across his face, "Bonita, I was so worried about you when you didn't come back. I came last night, and you weren't here." Josefina's face is very puzzled as Alejandro keeps talking. While he is talking, he is making sure the food he is cooking is being stirred and flipped. It appears to be some authentic Mexican rice dish, seafood, and a fresh salad.

"What time is it?" Josefina asks as she heads for the table to sit down. Then she looks at the clock and sees that it is quarter after six. "Yeah, I'm fine. I got back late this morning. I didn't think I would make the night." Josefina shows Alejandro her hands.

"Oh, Josefina, those look horrible. Are you alright?" Alejandro asks.

"Sure, now. They were full of splinters. The real deep ones I had to dig out. They feel worse than they look."

Alejandro chuckles, "Well, then, you must be in pain."

"Shouldn't you be at work?" Josefina asks while they start eating.

"All businesses are closed today. The mayor has asked everyone to take the next two days off so they can fix the mess in the tunnel. When over twenty vehicles collide it sure makes a big mess. The tunnel coming into the city is still operational. They're just going to want to check for structure damage once they clear out the south."

*A Legend Awakens*

"Oh, yeah that." Josefina sinks her head. "How many people died Alejandro?"

Alejandro can see the sadness in her eyes, so he tries to be honest but careful, "The final tally isn't in yet. But the unofficial total is a lot lower than you would imagine. Most of the traffic stopped after the motorcycle hit the wall. The two gas tankers caused the most damage. Those were two of the big explosions. A lot of smoke from them…"

"How many?"

"As of now, they have found just nineteen bodies. The fire was immense. It's not your fault. Miss Downey told the city how heroic you were in saving her from the kidnapping. She did you a favor. She said you went into the inferno to save the others."

With a look of guilt and anguish, Josefina sadly says, "It's my fault. Innocent people perished. I was stupid to think I could do this. I need to just leave. Turn myself in."

Alejandro with sternness, "What do you expect when you fight a war against the Peligrosa? Innocent people will die. Don't be so naive." Josefina looks surprised by Alejandro's retort. He continues his lecture. "In less than one week you have single-handedly shown weakness in the brick wall strength of the Peligrosa and you have disrupted the mayor's plans. You have brought back forgotten hope to the thousands of people that you are now protecting. 'Zorra' is everywhere. People are painting over the Peligrosa graffiti bringing hope back." Alejandro takes in a deep breath to control his breathing. "Yes, innocent people have sadly perished, but you can't let their deaths stop what you have started. Innocent people always die when there is greed. You can never stop that. Let their deaths mean something. No one blames you for this. The true target of your rage is the mayor. You and he have a lot more in common than you know."

Josefina is disgusted with being told she has things in common with the mayor then bites back, "I have nothing in common with that evil man. He hates the people he has been sworn to take care of. He is the Peligrosa…. how dare you compare me to him!"

Alejandro puts his hands up in a "calm down" motion and tries to gently reassure her, "You have misinterpreted what I said."

"I don't think I have. You said I had a lot in common with him, and the last I knew common meant the same."

"It does. I don't mean traits. I mean you have a past that is in common."

"I know we do. He is in charge of the Peligrosa and they killed my family."

"Your past with him goes much further than just you and him. Your families have a long history."

Completely lost with the current situation and the occurrences of the past few days, Josefina gives up. "Alright, there are way too many things happening that I need answers to."

Alejandro pulls the food off his fork with his teeth and chews it around a bit. Takes a great gulp of his drink and asks, "What do you want to know Bonita?"

Josefina puts her utensils down, raises her hands palms up, and looks around, "First of all… how did you get in here? You gathered my things the other night and now you are here. And what do you know about my family's history?" She said, pointing at him.

"The immediate answer to those two questions will cause you to ask me many more questions." He looks her directly into her eyes and says, "I tried telling you the other night. You were so tired when you arrived. You fell asleep. You mentioned the other night that you feel you don't exist. And it's true you don't."

She concentrates hard, "What do you know? I want to know it all. I'm sick and tired of being confused. This connection between me and Bigler you just mentioned and why don't I exist."

"Well, you don't exist is simple enough… it's because I hid you."

"You hid me?"

*A Legend Awakens*

"Yes, now finish your meal. It's made with a lot of proteins and calories. You need to get well nourished. I will give you an abridged explanation of everything. It seems I'm the only one who knows it all. I want no interruptions from you… okay?"

"Okay."

"I mean it. Let me tell you the way I tell you. NO interruptions."

Josefina did not want to argue or fight. She just wants answers. "Okay, Alejandro. I promise I won't interrupt."

Alejandro gets up from the table to start picking up the dishes while he begins his explanation, "While I start this explanation you will surely have more questions. Don't worry though I will get to answering them."

Josefina nods in acceptance, "I know, I promise I'll let you finish."

"I will start with what you are familiar with, the fire. The Peligrosa burned your house down. Allegedly the common knowledge is that the Peligrosa are working for Mayor Bigler. So, if we put one and one together, then it is safe to assume Mayor Bigler wanted your family dead. And why you ask? It is simple, he wants revenge. It's sad because the revenge he wants has nothing to do with you personally. In fact, he doesn't even know you're alive. And for the moment he thinks 'Zorra' is dead as well. This is a good thing. The mayor has no idea who any of your departed family members were. He just knew the name, Murrieta. The Murrieta family and the Bigler family have crossed paths during the history of California many years ago." Alejandro explains the history and how unfair it was that the Five Joaquins were rounded up and blamed for most of the crimes of thievery during the Gold Rush. He also told Josefina that her ancestor, Joaquin Murrieta, was one of the Five Joaquins. He connected the dots for her, connecting Governor Bigler, Captain Love, and Joaquin Murrieta to their direct descendants; Mayor Bigler, Captain Love, and Josefina Murrieta.

Alejandro goes into detail about the mayor's taste for gold while he finishes the dishes. He then leads Josefina to the living room.

Once in the living room, Alejandro has Josefina sit on the couch then he walks around the room explaining how he knows where she lives, "Now to tackle another subject… this apartment and all its décor. After your home was burnt to the foundation, I came back to see what I could salvage for you. The only thing that wasn't burnt and the Peligrosa never touched was a small garage out behind your house." Memories flood back to Josefina instantly reminding her of the garage from her youth. She remembers spending time there with her older brother. She wants to start telling Alejandro about all the boxes and the old car under a tarp that her brother was working on but never got to fix, but as she promised Alejandro earlier, she remains silent. Alejandro continues, "In that garage were a high-mileage convertible, tools, and many boxes of beautiful Mexican décor." Alejandro points out all the Mexican decorations around the apartment.

Alejandro sits down beside Josefina and continues, "I gathered all those items and brought them here. I brought the key to this apartment and the gold medallion hanging around your neck to you ten years ago when you were at the hospital. My instincts knew then that I had to make you disappear. I personally removed your DNA information from the computer system. My old girlfriend, Kayla, erased all information about you from the hospital's database. My cousin, Evee, God rest her soul, was nice enough to take care of you for six years and then my old partner, Robert, his son, Cameron, let you go to his gym where you now work. There is no record of your existence. I hid you here in plain sight so that the mayor couldn't get to you." Alejandro stops talking and is waiting for Josefina to say something. Josefina wiggles a bit and motions to her lips showing that she is being quiet like he had asked. Finally realizing it, Alejandro, says, "You may speak now."

*A Legend Awakens*

Josefina clutches onto the black medallion around her neck then looks at Alejandro and states, "So, you're my 'uncle'."

"Oh no, I'm not your uncle."

"I know, it's what the landlord said when I confronted him."

"Oh, yes, the landlord. He loves his cash. I've known him for years. He's made sure you have been okay. He keeps me informed whenever I pay him. That's it? Nothing else?"

"Oh no, I have more questions…" Josefina starts thinking of more questions, but she really can't think of any, "well, no. You actually did clear a lot for me. I'm just confused about why you didn't let me know. Why you kept it a secret from me."

"I wanted to tell you, but I had no clue how you would react. When I would talk to Evee, she would tell me how quiet and well-adjusted you had become. Not to mention very bright and athletic. I opened my restaurant and had her bring you to the gym and come by for lunch just so I could keep an eye on you."

Josefina, with regret and a broken heart, sorrowfully says, "Sorry about your cousin's death. I didn't know. I loved her. I never told her, but she took great care of me. When I found out the other day what the Peligrosa did, I became even more enraged. I just found out. I regret never going back to visit."

Alejandro leans forward and puts his hand on her knee, "Evee was a great woman. She loved you like a daughter. She told me so herself. She knows you loved her."

Josefina smiles a bit, sighs, and then asks, "You must hate Bigler and his men as much as I do. What do we do now?"

"We…," Alejandro surprisingly asks, "I thought Zorra was carrying on this burden by herself?"

An astute Josefina slyishly smiles, "Apparently you have been helping her for the last ten years." Josefina points around to all the exercise equipment in her apartment.

"Evee told me how much you enjoyed your visits to the gym so I figured I would furnish this apartment with the things you like."

With her left hand still clutching to her medallion she asks, "So this is gold? Why is it black?"

"I painted it so no one would try stealing it. You see, it's the gold that drives the mayor crazy. Like I told you earlier, he feels it's his."

"This is the last of my family's gold?"

"That and the gold cross you saved. Your ancestor, Joaquin, donated the gold he stole… Let me rephrase that. The gold he took back was melted into the Church's prize possession. You can bet anything, the Peligrosa will be going after that again."

Josefina, remembering that the Peligrosa has a trailer load of something to be picked up in just under six hours urgently changed the subject, "The Peligrosa, I have to go back to the railyard. They have a deadline to meet tonight."

Alejandro with a well-warranted concern about her condition, "Are you physically ready for it tonight? Maybe you should sit this one out."

"I can't sit it out. They have a big deadline to meet. If they miss it some guy named Serpente will be pissed and send his people to take on the Peligrosa. If I can stop this delivery, then Serpente will wipe out the rest of the Peligrosa. I have no choice but to do it."

"What's your plan, bonita?"

Josefina smiles when she answers, "I haven't had one yet. Just winging as I go. Pure stupid luck has worked so far."

Alejandro chuckles again, then asks, "What is this urgent matter?"

"A shipment of some sort… I heard them discussing it needs to be ready at one in the morning on Wednesday. Today is Tuesday, so it's happening…" she looks at the clock again to see it is almost seven-thirty at night, "I got to be there ready for it."

"If this thing is as huge as you think it is, then there will be a lot of guns. You can believe Ricardo will have patrols keeping a lookout for you. Even though they think you burned in the fire, there has been no body found. Ricardo is not as ignorant as you may think. He will be cautious. Is this shipment going by train?"

Josefina concentrates for a bit then says, "They said they will have a truck to come and pick up the trailer."

Very confident Alejandro says, "Perfecto intel, Bonita. We don't have to go to the station. We can ambush the driver when he leaves. There is only one exit out of that railyard by truck."

"Wait a minute. What's this we? It's going to just be me."

"Not on this one. Do you know how to drive a tractor-trailer? I do. Going in will be suicide. Ambushing the driver after he leaves city limits is the best way to handle this. And I have all the tools you need." Alejandro and Josefina start hatching out their plan.

## CHAPTER 18

# MEETING OF THE MINDS

"What an amazing bittersweet turn of events! On the one hand, I'm happy that Zorra is dead. On the other hand, I'm quite sad that I don't have her head. And on the third hand, I AM OUTRAGED that you dumb-asses didn't get rid of Ms. Downey!" Mayor Bigler is sitting behind the desk in his penthouse office eating his dinner as he loudly discusses the recent activities with Captain Love and Ricardo. "Your inept men managed to let her get saved and got themselves killed. Worst of all, we lost a perfectly good van. I guess I'll just have the taxpayers buy another one. So, Captain Love, any luck on her remains. I would like her head, even if it is… a little well done."

"Come on, John, everything was completely destroyed. There are no remains of anything."

"That's mayor," he then shifts his focus to Ricardo, "how about you? Any luck on finding Ms. Downey?"

Ricardo smiles at Captain Love when he says, "No, Mayor Bigler. After her telling the heroics of Zorra, she disappeared. Even my guys in the police department have no clue."

Captain Love gives a little chuckle and under his breadth mutters, "Your guys. Your guys are as useless as the one who leads them."

Ricardo snaps back, "My men are one-hundred percent loyal to me! Can you say that about yours? In fact, your men are more loyal to me than to you!"

"Shove it up your ass Ricardo before you get what's coming!"

As Ricardo and Harry stand "alpha male" staring each other down, the mayor gets off his chair, adjusts his pants to tuck his shirt in, and approaches the men. He squeezes in between them and puts one arm around each of their shoulders, "Now gentlemen, we're best friends here. No need to ruin everything over petty who-follows-who. We all know everyone does what I say so I want us all to make up." John pulls them in closer as if they just had a group hug. "There, wasn't that great?" He pats them on their backs and gives them a shove away from him as he turns back to his desk. John readjusts the napkin on his lap and then starts chewing on a steak. Full mouthed he still clearly announces, "I'm still sad I don't have her head. Oh well, maybe with that troublesome Zorra gone you two can finally manage to get that beautiful cross to me."

Captain Love, annoyed with everything the mayor says and does, rolls his eyes. Then with a sly smirk towards Ricardo says, "That might have to wait, John. I heard rumors of something big happening down at the railyard. Your lackey, Ricardo, might be able to fill us in on more details. Would you care to enlighten us, Ricardo?"

Mayor Bigler switches his attention towards Ricardo. Ricardo not wanting the mayor to know of his large money transaction quickly chimes in, "I don't know what he's talking about. It's my place and I know everything that goes on there."

"Wrong Ricardo," John swallows then finishes, "This is my city and I would know if something was happening. Captain Love, why are you trying to start something here? We just hugged and became best friends again."

"I'm not trying to start something, John. I have very reliable information that Ricardo is up to something."

"That's MAYOR, Captain, what is supposed to be happening and when?"

Ricardo, starting to sweat a bit, looks angrily in the captain's direction. Harry then says, "I don't know exactly what or when I was just informed that something big was occurring sometime soon."

Ricardo relaxes and sneers. The mayor then says, "Again, Captain, if something was happening in MY city, I would know what it is. Let's get back to this cross. Captain Love, I need you to make sure your men are busy. With that new alarm system the church has, your guys will need to be busy for when Ricardo leads his men to successfully acquire my gold. I want this done by midweek. I'll have all the businesses closed for a mourning period so this should give you empty streets for a quick getaway. Captain Love will make sure his police force is responding elsewhere and I will have my gold. It's a perfect plan."

A perturbed Harry says, "That's not a plan John, that's an idea."

Ricardo edging on Harry with his fake ass-kissing says, "It sounds like a good plan Mayor. I'll have my men cause some chaos on the other end of the city keeping the police busy and then we'll swoop in and take the cross."

The mayor smiling loves what he just heard, "Swoop! That's it! We'll use my helicopter!"

"You have a helicopter?" Harry asked.

"Of course I do. I have been letting the police station use it," the mayor says with a sly smile.

Again, rolling his eyes, "You wanted this done discretely and now you want the police to use their helicopter to deliver it to you."

Ricardo then agrees with John, "That would work fine. It will be easier to connect a harness to the cross. Within minutes it would be airlifted to your penthouse. It will be quick and simple. The pilot is one of ours, right?"

The mayor wipes his mouth and says, "No, the police pilot has been unapproachable. But my nephew can fly. I paid for his flying lessons. I'll have him go see you, Captain. You and he can plan how you will get him to the helicopter. In the meantime, I want to finish my meal in peace. Good night gentlemen." The mayor escorts Ricardo and Captain Love to the door.

CHAPTER 19

# SPOILED PLANS

It's twelve-thirty Wednesday morning and waiting on the cusp of the city just half a mile away from the railyard, Zorra and Deputy Alejandro are keeping their wits about them. They are parked in a black Nissan 350 Z convertible with the top up. This is the same convertible Deputy Alejandro rescued ten years ago. Zorra sitting in the passenger's seat impatiently says, "Are you sure this is going to work?"

"Of course it will. If you're carrying a shipment of something illegal and you're a professional at your job, you will remain calm and not break any rules. You're not going to want to make a scene."

Zorra then looks over at Deputy Alejandro and with a great chuckle and smirk says, "Your uniform, it's a little small."

"I never thought I would wear this again." Deputy Alejandro's old deputy uniform is a little snug. The last time he wore it was when he rescued Josefina from the fire. The injury he sustained to his leg forced his retirement. Looking in the rearview mirror, Deputy Alejandro looks at himself sitting in the driver seat of the car that he had found in Josefina's family garage. It is a high-mileage convertible, but the engine is just as reliable as the day it was made. Nissan sure makes a great engine. This sports car is an automatic 2005 Nissan 350 Z Touring Roadster. It is black with black leather seats. Alejandro finished the reconditioning of this fun ride from where Josefina's brother had been interrupted… with a few alterations. Deputy Alejandro awakens out of his quick flashback just in time. A trailer-less truck is coming up the road headed towards the railyard. He then taps Zorra on the leg, "see… right on time. If the trailer is ready, he should be back through here in fifteen minutes."

"Why don't we stop him now? We could then pick up the trailer."

Deputy Alejandro reassuringly says, "That just won't do. I'm sure they will want to see the credentials of the driver. They might already know what he looks like. Let's stick to this plan, it will work just fine." He then goes over the plan with her again. "When the truck comes back by, this is the only way out so he will come back, we will let him pass a distance before we follow. After he makes it out of Perilous City that is when I'll turn on the lights," Deputy Alejandro points to the dashboard-mounted police lights and continues, "I will then pull him over. Let me assess the situation first."

"What if he shoots you?" enquires a worried Zorra.

"Don't worry I have a vest on. My gun will be at my side ready to pull out."

"The truck sits higher than you. He won't be shooting your vest. It's your head I'm worried about."

"Again, don't worry. This will go without a hitch. I will get him to come down then I will handcuff him and leave him on the side of the highway. You just flip this switch here to turn off the police lights and follow me. No other heroics… got it!"

"Where are we bringing it?"

"There is an old unused weigh station ten miles south of the city right before the interstate exchange heading east. We will open it up there to see what we are hauling. From that point, we will decide what we will do with the trailer."

A concerned and nervous Zorra disappointedly says, "I think now is a good time to let you know I have never driven a car before."

Deputy Alejandro wide-eyed turns his head looking at Zorra and replies, "You got to be kidding me, bonita. When I told you about this plan five hours ago, then would have been a good time to tell me. It's a good thing it's automatic. Wait a second, you were driving a motorcycle just the other day."

"I found that extremely difficult and scary."

Deputy Alejandro gives a short tutorial, "The car has two more wheels, so it is twice as easy. Make sure you put your foot on the brake before you shift this into drive. See it will say, 'D', up here. Then press the gas to go. Be careful, I added a turbo and increased the horsepower. This baby opens up! Your headlights are here. Most importantly don't be nervous. Don't destroy this like you did the motorcycle. I mean it."

"Very funny, I didn't do it on purpose. I'm shocked I didn't wreck it sooner."

Bright lights beam into the rearview mirror. Deputy Alejandro glances in his side mirror and says, "Here we go."

The truck with its trailer shakes the Z as it passes. About twenty seconds pass before Deputy Alejandro starts the Z to follow him. Catching up to the truck is not an issue for the very fast Z. Within moments they are two-hundred yards behind the trailer. The traffic out of the city at one in the morning is practically non-existent. It is an opportune time for the truck driver to leave Perilous City and head back to New York. One mile after exiting the tunnel they left the city limits and were no longer on a shared highway, Deputy Alejandro turned the dash-mounted police lights on. It took a few moments but just as planned the trailer's right turn signal light came on and the truck's down-shifting noise was audible. A minute later the truck is pulled to the side of the highway and the airbrakes make its sssssssssssssshhhhhhhhhh sound.

"Be careful." Zorra cautions.

"Everything will be fine. NOT A SCRATCH!" Deputy Alejandro pulls himself out of the Z. He purposely keeps the bright lights on so that the driver can't see him approach. He hobbles to the trailer and extends his left arm with the baton and taps it on the door. His right hand is on his revolver ready to pull it out.

The driver lowers his window and asks in his East Coast accent, "What can I do faw yaw offisaw?"

Deputy Alejandro says, "Do you know why I pulled you over?"

"Not a clue offisaw. I was goin the speed limit and usin my signal lights. I wasn't swoovin. I haven't got a clue."

"You have two taillights out. Please exit the truck with your license and driver's log."

The driver thinks to himself, *that stupid Ricardo. He said everything was ready.* He opened the door and came down with his license and log. "Here yaw go offisaw." The driver looks closely at the non-fitting uniform and notices the county badge. He then confusingly says, "or shouldz I say deputy?"

Deputy Alejandro notices the confusion on his face and then grabs at the driver's extended arm and within half a second has him pinned face-first to the ground. Deputy Alejandro places his knee into the driver's back with his right arm twisted behind. Sure enough, as he planned the driver is handcuffed. Still at a complete lost, the driver is dragged to the side of the highway out of harm's way.

"What yaw doin this faw?!" The driver yells.

"You know." Deputy Alejandro limps back to the cab, gives a thumbs-up to Zorra, and climbs into the cab. After assessing the controls Deputy Alejandro commences driving the truck down the highway.

Zorra however is not satisfied. She runs over to the driver who is struggling to get to his feet. She pushes him back down on his back, "Ow!! That hurts." He then gets a good look at Zorra and asks, "What the hell? What is it, Halloween?"

"Shut up." She bends down and lifts his bangs hoping to see a tattoo. She then asks, "Are you a Peligrosa?"

"Naw bitch. I don't woyk for that two-bit small outfit. I woyk for Mistah Sawpente, HE, yaw don't wanna cwoss."

"Well too bad, we did!" A confident Zorra exclaims.

In his New York cockiness, "Well missy, yaw might wanna rethink that."

"Now why would we do that? This is my city and organized crime is no longer welcomed here. And you can tell your Mr. Serpente that."

"Oh, boy… aw yaw naive… awganized crime is nevah welcomed but it is sure alive and well. I tell yaw what missy, it is always there and there ain't nothin you can do about it."

"That's where you're wrong. We have your truck, so it is over for you. What are you hauling?" Zorra gives him a good whack on his head with the back of her hand.

The driver gives off a great hearty laugh and then warns, "Like I said missy, we aint no two-bit outfit. As soon as the police lights came on, I hit the emehgency switch. The way I figyaw it, yaw cop buddy gots about five mo minutes befaw Mistah Sawpente sends in mo muscle."

Zorra looks a little confused and asks, "What do you mean?"

"Do yaws actually think he would send in one man? If somethin goes wrong, like bein pulled ovaw, we have anothaw team to move in and get it back."

"How can you get it back if you don't know where it is?"

"Mistah Sawpente has all his vehicles connected with a GPS trackaw. So, he will find it and yaw friend. I kind of hope now yaw friend makes it hawd faw us to get it back, yaw won't want to know what happenz if we don't get it back."

Zorra, more perturbed, smacks him again but harder, "What will happen?"

He shakes it off a bit and smiles with his answer, "If we can't have it no one can."

Zorra thinking the worse, "What will happen?"

He laughs and says, "Yaw pawtnaw saved my life keepin me out of theyaw. That truck's got enough explosives that noooo body will be able to identify nothin."

Zorra springs to her feet and darts back to the 350 Z leaving the driver behind. Zorra quickly remembers what Deputy Alejandro told her about driving. She puts her foot on the brake and puts the Z in drive. She quickly pounced on the accelerator and launched forward without checking to see if the traffic was clear. She almost loses control as she weaves back and forth trying to avoid the car she just cut off and zips right by the truck driver who just managed to roll off the road into the shoulder.

Deputy Alejandro pulls the truck off the interstate onto the exit ramp of the unused weigh station. He climbs out of the cab and looks behind him to see if Zorra has arrived yet. "I hope she's alright." Deputy Alejandro limps to the back of the trailer and sees there are two deadbolts keeping it locked. "Come on Zorra the bolt cutters are in the Z." A few moments pass and Deputy Alejandro hears a familiar exhaust tone. The Z comes flying down the ramp screeching its wheels to a dead stop. Zorra jumps out of the Z. She hears Deputy Alejandro yell, "Put it in park!!!"

Zorra yells back at him, "What!?" Then she sees Deputy Alejandro hobbling fast towards the Z to cut it off before it passes him. He opens the door and using his one good leg hops down into the driver seat.

After he stops the Z and puts it in park, Deputy Alejandro extends his arm out of the window and waves Zorra over. She rushes over to him. He calmly says, "You see, the P is for park. You have to use that once the car has stopped and you want to get out. I see she is in one piece. What took you so long? You should have been right behind me." He pulls himself up and out of the Z.

Zorra panting from her heart-thumping very fast car ride urgently warns, "Alejandro, we have to go! There is a GPS tracking device on the truck and it is packed with explosives! If they can't get it the whole thing is blowing up."

"Whoa, whoa, whoa, slow down. How do you know that?"

"I interrogated the driver. That's why I'm late."

"He probably just said that to scare you so you would leave."

"He said at the moment he saw the police lights he hit the warning button."

Deputy Alejandro and Zorra head back to the truck. He climbs back in and sees a small red light blinking in front of his right knee. "That might be it. What else did he say?"

"He said about ten minutes ago that Mr. Serpente would know something was up in five minutes and would send in the muscle. If they can't get the truck, then the whole thing would blow up, leaving nothing behind."

Deputy Alejandro got down halfway and looked under the driver's seat. His eyes widen then he tells Zorra, "Back up bonita. This thing is rigged with something I've never seen before. You said if they don't get the truck they would blow it. They haven't tried getting it yet, so it's safe to say it won't blow up anytime soon." Deputy Alejandro gets out, unhooks the power and airlines then starts winding down the trailer legs to hold it in place.

Zorra asks, "What are you doing?"

"Leaving the trailer and taking the truck. They're tracking the truck, not the merchandise."

"This isn't part of the plan." Zorra nervously says.

Deputy Alejandro jokingly replies, "No plans seem to be working for you thus far, so I figure I'd give it a shot." Deputy Alejandro climbs back behind the steering wheel of the truck. He then drives the truck out from underneath the trailer. Deputy Alejandro looks out the window and says to Zorra, "About fifteen more miles south is the canyon. Pick me up there." Deputy Alejandro races out of the abandoned weigh station very fast toward his next destination.

Not liking any of this, Zorra yells, "Assuming you make it! I hate not knowing what's going on." She runs to the Z. Feeling claustrophobic Zorra sees the button to open the top. She hits the button. Nothing happens. The car is not even running. She looks around and sees the key in the ignition, twists it and it starts. She doesn't let go of the key right away then she hears an odd sound and releases the key. The Z is purring. She pushes the roof button, and nothing happens. "Damn!" Then she looks at the brake light flashing. She puts her foot on the brake and pushes the button again. This time it makes a noise. She sees the roof try to lift then stops. "It's catching on something." She looks up to see a gray handle. "That's got to be it." Zorra flips the handle then the roof lifts a bit. She puts her foot back on the brake, holds the roof button and it opens completely. The moment everything stops moving she removes her finger from the button. The roof was completely hidden in the back. "I like this." She said with a smile. Zorra puts it in drive and launches herself once again in the direction Deputy Alejandro went.

It doesn't take Zorra long to catch up. Deputy Alejandro was behind three other trucks, his being the only one without a trailer. She pulls up next to him and yells, "What's the plan!"

Deputy Alejandro yells back, "The canyon is up ahead! I figure we will make this jump the guardrails. If it explodes on contact, they will assume everything went up with it! It will give us some time to get another truck to get the trailer!"

Zorra shakes her head in disagreement, "Not a good idea! How are you getting out of the truck in time before it goes over?!"

Not thinking of that one well enough, Deputy Alejandro yells back, "Good point! I'm pulling over!" Deputy Alejandro slows down the truck, takes it off the road, and parks it on the shoulder. Zorra stops right behind him. She sits in the Z as she sees Deputy Alejandro fidgeting with something then he hurriedly exits the truck and wobbles towards the Z, "Scoot over I'm driving."

"What's going on?" Zorra moves to the passenger seat.

Deputy Alejandro tosses her a small device then gets in the Z, "Much easier without the roof."

"What's this?"

"That's the tracking device. I'm heading back to the city."

"What?"

"The city, I have to get another truck." Deputy Alejandro speeds back up and heads for the interstate exchange. After a few minutes and three cloverleaf turns, they're headed north towards the city.

"But they can follow us."

"They sure can. They are looking for a truck and trailer not a convertible. No signs of them yet, keep your eyes out. I have a feeling they will be zipping by us soon. They can't be too far." Deputy Alejandro wedged themselves between two tractor-trailers. A few miles outside of the city right before the tunnel, several black SUVs with New York plates pass the tractor-trailer that is behind the Z then pass them. As the first SUV gets to the front of the tractor-trailer in front of them blue lights come on. "That's got to be them. They think one of these trucks has the device."

"What are you going to do now?"

"Head into the city of course," Deputy Alejandro pulls into the passing lane and zips past the SUVs which are now pulling over the two tractor-trailers. He looks into the rearview mirror while Zorra turns in the seat on her knees watching what's happening. Both trucks pull over and that is the last they see of them because they now enter the tunnel. Deputy Alejandro gets halfway through the tunnel when he says to Zorra, "They must know by now that what they're looking for is not on those trailers. They should be coming after us again. We can't hide in the tunnel."

Zorra then says, "Let's not let this leave the tunnel then." Now sitting properly in her seat again, she flings the device at the wall of the tunnel. "There, what the wall didn't do the continuous traffic will finish."

Deputy Alejandro smiles, "I was thinking about leaving it at the mayor's doorstep but that works too."

"Oh, man, that would have been great Alejandro. You need to communicate better."

Deputy Alejandro quips back, "You need to be less spontaneous."

About fifteen minutes pass and Deputy Alejandro brings the Z into what looks like an inner-city junkyard. He puts the roof back up on the Z and finishes it off with the dark-shaded windows closing. Zorra says, "Can't we keep the roof down?"

"I don't want anyone to see you. Remember the mayor thinks you're dead."

Zorra scouting the area, "What are we doing here?"

"An old buddy of mine owns this place. He'll have a truck I can borrow with no questions asked. You go home and get some rest."

"I want to get the trailer too?"

"I'm not getting the trailer yet."

"Sure you are. I'm not stupid."

"Really, I'm not. I'm going to go back to my place and rest too. It's at an abandoned weigh station. No one will know it's there. Besides, I'm opening the restaurant in a few hours anyways. I'll pick you up tonight. Take the Z and go back to your home." He tosses the keys to Zorra.

Zorra catches the keys and states the obvious, "My apartment. I don't have a place to park this. I don't think this will be safe left on the road."

Deputy Alejandro, once again with the answer, "Surprise, you do have a place there to park it. I pay for the garage space too. Press that button on the mirror and the garage will open. Don't forget to put it in park. P is for park. See you later."

"Fine," Zorra pouts, climbs into the driver seat, and leaves Deputy Alejandro behind.

Deputy Alejandro goes to the entrance of the building that leads to the gated junkyard. A few moments go by before he is let in. About twenty minutes pass when the gate opens and Deputy Alejandro leaves the premises in a very old-looking semi-truck heading back to the interstate. He turns the radio on and hears there has been a massive explosion wiping out the southbound lanes about twenty miles south of the city. Traffic will be routed again to the northbound side.

Deputy Alejandro ignores the cones and drives the truck towards the abandoned weigh station. To his amazement, when Deputy Alejandro pulls up to the abandoned trailer, he sees the Z with the top down and Zorra waiting for him. Zorra's obnoxious grin is gleaming. Deputy Alejandro passes her shaking his head and then backs up to the trailer. He climbs out saying to Zorra, "I thought I told you to get some rest."

"You also told me you were coming for this tonight. Since I figured you were being deceitful with that you also meant the opposite when you said you wanted me to go home and get some rest."

"It's just a simple pick up and go. What gave it away? How did you know I was coming?" Deputy Alejandro connects the trailer and starts winding the trailer support legs.

"Nothing is simple with the Peligrosa. Don't forget businesses were supposed to be closed one more day since the tunnel catastrophe. So, you weren't opening the restaurant like you said. That was the giveaway. The sun is coming up. Don't you think that trailer will stick out like a sore thumb in the city? There's no graffiti on it."

"I don't think they're looking for it anymore. Did you hear the news? They exploded the truck."

*A Legend Awakens*

Zorra holds out the bolt cutters and hands them to Deputy Alejandro, "Shut up! That's why the emergency vehicles zipped past. I hope no one got hurt. We did just leave it on the shoulder."

Deputy Alejandro knows Zorra is upset and correct. He isn't going to press the issue anymore. He takes the cutters and breaks the locks. He hands the cutters back to her and moves the latches to open the doors. He swings them wide open. Six-foot-tall stacks of palletized brown packages went all the way to the front of the trailer.

Zorra asks, "What do you think it is?"

"Only one way to find out," Deputy Alejandro takes out a knife and pokes the package closest to him. A very fine white powder is on his knife.

"Cocaine?" Zorra wonders.

"Could be..." Deputy Alejandro puts a bit on his tongue then spits it out immediately, "heroin."

"Heroin? They're making heroin at the railyard! I have to stop that!"

"Hold on bonita. It's time to get the authorities involved. This is now a DEA matter... interstate trade of an illegal substance. They'll lock up the entire gang."

"I don't want them locked up. I want them dead."

Deputy Alejandro looks Zorra in her eyes, "You can't kill them all. It won't bring back your family."

"It will bring back peace to me."

Deputy Alejandro and Zorra keep rehashing her feelings versus justice and not paying attention to the line of New York-plated SUVs approaching them. Deputy Alejandro stops talking and holds his hand up to Zorra telling her to quiet. He then sees the first set of headlights and yells, "Get in the Z and get the hell out of here. Serpente's men are here." Deputy Alejandro runs to the truck which is already hooked to the trailer and climbs in. Zorra has already passed him as he floors it while the other SUVs follow behind.

Zorra takes the lead with Deputy Alejandro following right behind. He keeps weaving back and forth preventing the SUVs from getting in front. He figures they aren't shooting at his tires or at him since they didn't destroy the shipment, they probably want some of it back. Up ahead is the massive hole in the ground that was left from the explosion earlier. A few state troopers are there assessing the situation as Zorra takes the Z off-road on the left shoulder and pulls it back onto the highway. Deputy Alejandro does the same maneuver but not as graceful, and the right back wheels of the trailer go off the road and into the blasted hole. The right side of the axle hits hard and he pulls it through. Two of the pallets on the back of the open trailer topple out and smash open on the interstate causing two of the seven SUVs to fall into the hole. The state troopers are at a complete loss of what to do. A couple of troopers stay behind to see about the New Yorkers and the other two squad cars follow the chase.

Zorra backs off and rides along Deputy Alejandro since the SUV traffic slowed down a bit. She figured now was the time to speak to him before he started weaving again. She yells up to him, "Déjà Vu! What now?! The ramps to go back north are coming up?"

Deputy Alejandro with sincerity this time yells, "Stay close to me! The overpass over the canyon is coming soon! The cruise is set and I'll yank the wheel to the right when we get on it. At that point I'll jump in the Z." He then raises the window so he won't have to hear Zorra's objection.

Zorra looks into her rearview mirror and sees SUVs and two troopers approaching the truck fast. She has no doubt they'll be able to catch up to the truck, but she can't lose them. Deputy Alejandro's truck is governed at eighty-miles-per-hour and has no chance of outrunning any of them. Zorra slows down naively thinking she can run them off the road. The two lead SUVs come on each side of her with the remaining three behind her. At this point, she realizes how small her car is in comparison to the large SUVs.

Zorra looks to her left and sees the passenger of that SUV pointing a machine gun at her. "Oh shit!" She floors the accelerator and is pegged back into her seat as she takes off like a rocket. The man in the SUV opens fire and a couple of rounds hit the rear driver-side fender as she launches twenty yards ahead with no issues in seconds. A few of the rounds from the machine guns did hit the front wheel of the SUV that was to her right. She sees that SUV veer off while saying, "Organized crime might be everywhere and they might have bigger guns, but they're just as stupid as the Peligrosa."

They are now at the overpass. Zorra pulls up next to Deputy Alejandro as he is holding up his pointer telling her to wait. She gets relieved because she thinks he has decided not to do it. He then lowers his window and yells out, "Not at eighty! I'm going down to forty right now! Get ready!" He slowed down so fast causing the SUV that is directly behind him to turn his wheel abruptly to the left that he startles the other SUV driver which causes him to slam his bakes sending the driver behind him right into his rear and causing a crippling collision taking out two more SUV's leaving two SUV's and two troopers.

Zorra sees Deputy Alejandro's thumb come up, she sees the door open, and then sees Deputy Alejandro on the side of the truck with the door now shut steering the truck. While the truck starts to turn right, she follows as closely as she dares to. Deputy Alejandro judges the distance and, in a few milliseconds later, his feet are in the Z's passenger seat with his right arm holding onto the A-pillar for support and his left arm bracing on the back roll bar. He then slides into the seat and holds his chest for a bit. Zorra says, "That was amazing! Are you—" The semi hit the side guardrail bending it outward forced by the weight of the truck instantly tipping the trailer causing the trailer and the truck to drop over two hundred feet into the canyon. Zorra comes to a stop in the far left lane. She looks at Deputy Alejandro who is still holding his chest, "Are you alright?"

"Nunca más," he says white faced, "Nunca más." Deputy Alejandro then looks to see two SUVs and two troopers coming up alongside. Machine guns were being pointed their way. "Get us out of here!!"

Zorra floors it south leaving them behind instantly. "Wow, Alejandro, that was so cool, you were amazing, I can't believe you did that…"

Quite obviously nervous, Deputy Alejandro begs, "Get us home."

"Where is the next turning point? I have never been on this highway before." Not waiting for an answer, Zorra acts spontaneously, "I'll just go back the way we came." She pounces on the brakes and then squeals the wheels turning the Z around heading back north.

"What, what, what are you doing? You're going the wrong way!"

A smiley Zorra eagerly says, "I'm getting us back home. I hope you're not worried about me breaking the law now!"

"But the guys who want us dead are in that direction."

"There's only two left." Zorra confidently says.

As they head north, they see only two vehicles heading their way. They're just the two SUVs. Zorra zooms right by and she sees them turn in the rearview mirror. Deputy Alejandro tells her to slow down as they approach the troopers' cars at the point where the truck went off. Serpente's men had killed the troopers. Deputy Alejandro reaches into the front seat pocket and pulls out a revolver. Josefina recognizes it. It is the same kind as one of the ones she has taken from the Peligrosa. He says to her, "Let them get close." Deputy Alejandro turns in his seat and faces the SUVs. Instead of going for the driver first, he shoots at the first SUV putting a hole through the windshield on the passenger side and taking out one. He then takes out the driver with one more shot. Leaving one SUV left. At this point, the passenger points his gun out the window to start shooting but too late, a bullet whizzes through his head. Then a fleeting moment later, with another dead accurate shot from Deputy Alejandro, the other SUV heads off the road and down the embankment. That driver too is done.

An impressed Zorra exclaims, "WOW! Four shots, you're good! We're coming up to the crater."

Deputy Alejandro turns back around in his seat and faces forward. The troopers that stayed behind are slain as well. Their cars are missing and so aren't the passengers of the other SUVs. Deputy Alejandro quietly says, "They're done here. They're headed back East." Zorra makes it back onto the northbound lane and heads back to the city. She gets to the apartment where she parks the car in the garage. Before Deputy Alejandro takes a taxi back to his restaurant he says, "I know the day just started for everyone else, but you need your rest. I will bring you something to eat. Get some sleep."

Zorra removes her disguise to become Josefina again. After a quick bite to eat, Josefina sits back on the couch and instead of turning on the television she looks at all her décor and smiles about her family legacy and what she is now a part of… what she has always been a part of.

CHAPTER 20

# WHOSE CITY IS IT?

It's ten in the morning and above the smog and the anguish of the poor, Mayor Bigler wakes up with the sunshine brightening his penthouse. His penthouse is one of the very few places that are lucky enough to be graced with a morning stream of sunlight since it sits above the smog. He is completely oblivious to the events that happened while he was in a comforting sleep. If he wasn't afraid of heights, John would have looked out the window to see the same helicopters from the other night now south of the tunnel circling the canyon.

The mayor prepares himself in the same manner he does every morning; same routine, closet full of the same black suits, at the exact same time every day. He takes his elevator down to the parking garage where he is greeted by Peter, his driver. Mayor Bigler's chauffeured limousine pulls out of the parking garage from One Bigler Avenue. It crosses the road and enters the parking garage for Two Bigler Avenue. The mayor exits the car and heads to his work office where breakfast and today's newspaper are waiting for him.

John sits down behind the desk in a room that is an exact replica of his home office. He squirms in his chair until he is comfortable. The mayor unfolds his napkin and tucks it in his shirt like a bib.

Very happily he combines his over-easy eggs with his grits. John breaks up the bacon and sausage and mixes it in his heaping pile of breakfast bliss. He loads some of it between two slices of toast and starts chowing it down. As he is reaching for his orange juice, Mayor Bigler looks down at the newspaper. It is wrapped with a different band marked "special edition" and after reading the headline on the front page of the newspaper he spits the entire mouth full of food all over his desk and exclaims, "WHAT IN HELL IS THIS!"

SPECIAL EDITION ***ZORRA LIVES!*** SPECIAL EDITION

"This can't be! I was told she burnt in the tunnel!" The mayor presses a button on his intercom and announces into it, "Good Morning Kathy, would you please get me Captain Love! Pronto! Oh, and you must have made a mess in here when you brought me my breakfast. Food is all over the desk. Could you be a dear and come clean it up?" The mayor is looking at two newspapers on his desk. Kathy comes in with a rag and a spray bottle of cleaner and heads towards the mayor's desk. He asks his assistant, who is now cleaning up his mess, "Why do we have two papers? Is this 'special edition' one a joke?"

Kathy looks at it and says, "No joke sir. You didn't watch the news this morning? It's very important news. I guess the paper didn't want to miss out, so they made a special run just for her. Great news isn't it sir? Now you can still give her the 'key' to the city."

"Yeah," he says hesitantly, "great news. Just finish up cleaning your mess and get out. The moment Captain Love gets here send him in." The mayor, very distraught, reads the article.

### Heroine halts hoodlums harvesting heroin.

*By: Rea Peterman*

*Zorra defies the Peligrosa again! This time it came with a large bang! Speculations can only guess what caused a large crater to appear, completely wiping out the southbound lanes ten miles south of Perilous City. Early this morning many eyewitnesses reported seeing Zorra speeding south and then north on the interstate in a black convertible sports car with a "Z". Reports told to this paper; claims she ran a truck loaded with heroin off the interstate into the canyon. The 200-foot drop completely scattered the heroin upon impact and Mother Nature's wind gusts finished spreading the rest. The bags that held the heroin were labeled with the mark of the Peligrosa. Early estimates put a street value of 1.2 billion dollars on this failed shipment speculated as heading towards San Francisco. Several state troopers have disappeared. The DEA and the FBI have been called in for further investigation...*

"I can't read anymore!" The mayor hurls the paper across the room. "The DEA! The FBI! I don't want them here. I don't need them here. It happened outside the city limits anyway. They have no reason to come here." John presses the intercom button on his desk again and demands, "Kathy, I need Ricardo here too. I need him here now!" Half an hour goes by with a very distraught mayor pacing in his office. His major worry is Zorra and why she is not dead.

While the mayor is pacing in his office, Ricardo and Harry meet outside the mayor's office. Harry smiles and smugly asks Ricardo,

"Nothing big happening huh?" He said this in reference to their last meeting with the mayor and Ricardo telling him nothing was going on at the railyard.

"Shut up asshole!" Ricardo blowing smoke across to Harry asks, "Which one of my guys told you something was going down?"

"Ricardo my boy," Captain Love started saying while patting Ricardo on his shoulder, "I am the true eyes and ears of this city. You might be the muscle but I'm the brain that controls it." Harry opens the door to the mayor's office and says to Ricardo, "After you sir."

A very pissed mayor says to the men as they walk in, "It's about time you two arrived! What the hell is going on? The CIA, FBI, MIA, and other agencies have been calling my office and listen, look," the mayor points to the paper that is still scattered over the floor. He also motions to the television which is airing live footage of the hole in the interstate with a white-powdered covered canyon. This live footage overlaps with some cell phone footage of Zorra speeding away with some unrecognizable person in the passenger seat. "I wake up to this mess and can't finish eating my breakfast! They're saying the Peligrosa made this heroin? What do you have to say for yourself?"

Ricardo caving in quickly replies with his raspy voice, "Yeah, so what? We manufactured the heroin. We have always made it. What the hell do you think we were doing before you became mayor? I just stepped up the production. I'm a businessman. I give my services to those that pay."

Very upset John starts fuming. Harry just stays back enjoying the show, "I pay you! You live in MY city! You use MY materials! Because of you, BIG BROTHER now wants to investigate me. They want to investigate this…"

Ricardo steps up unafraid of the mayor and says, "Listen, don't worry, so what? They ain't got nothing on you. They're useless, besides, we're ready to take that big gold cross for you tonight."

The very witty Ricardo knows the mayor's hot buttons all too well. By mentioning the gold, he quickly distracts the mayor making him forget about his heroin making.

The mayor gets all excited and says, "Oh great, I'll need you, Ricardo, to be back at my home when my nephew flies my gold there. I'll need you and a few men to bring it into my office. I'll have it placed next to the cabinet. What are your plans for Zorra if she arrives?"

Ricardo sneers, "I've got something in the works to stop her."

Harry Love asks, "What's that? You haven't been able to slow her down and NOW you expect to stop her. From what I hear she is too quick and sly for you and your men."

A perturbed Ricardo confronts Harry, with, which to him, seems to be a solid plan, "You're correct Harry, I have noticed that she is too quick for anyone to stop her. I am done underestimating her. When the helicopter safely takes the cross away and if she is there, one of my vans will be loaded with enough dynamite Zorra, the church, and the rest of the block will be a memory."

A sad mayor blurts out, "But I won't get my head."

An irritated Captain Love pleads, "But what about all the innocent people that live on the block? You can't let this happen, John!"

Ricardo callously states, "Casualties of war, Harry, casualties of war." Then he chuckles a bit.

Angrily, the captain waves his finger and points sternly at both the mayor and Ricardo, "I don't want any part of this. My hands are clean. You two are insane. This has gone too far. You're willing to eliminate hundreds of people for gold." Harry starts his exit and abruptly marches towards the door.

The mayor quickly shouts to him, "You are correct Captain, we can't let that happen. That is too much. The explosives are out. Ricardo, just put your best shooters on the rooftops and pick her off. Captain, you happy now?"

Harry rolls his eyes and says, "You're still insane John."

Ignoring the lack of using his title, the mayor says to Harry, "Captain, I'll have my nephew meet you at the station at seven tonight."

"Whatever," the captain leaves the mayor's office.

The mayor changing his attitude goes over to Ricardo and says, "I love it! Blow the block up! If the captain doesn't like it, then it gets my stamp of approval."

An approving Ricardo reiterates, "So you want me to explode her if she shows?"

"Don't blow her up. I want her head. Well at least cut her head off before you blow her to smithereens. Even if she doesn't show up, explode the block. The rest of the city needs to live in fear. You know, for me to maintain control. Have your men spread word through the streets that something big is going to happen at the church. You need her there." A confident mayor heads back to his desk and looks at Ricardo. "What are you waiting for? Get the hell out of my office."

"Very good sir," Ricardo leaves very happily.

Ricardo makes it back to the railyard to find visitors there. He sees a couple of New York-plated SUVs parked next to his abode. Ricardo is pretty sure he knows who they are. Once he opens the door, a couple of Peligrosa try to warn him that a few of Mr. Serpente's men are there. Ricardo lifts his hand up stopping them in their tracks and says, "Yeah, yeah, I know. Two of their vehicles are parked outside." He then looks at the four men standing there, blows out his smoke, and asks, "What can I do for ya's gentlemen?"

The one man he recognizes, the driver that was pulled over by Alejandro, speaks up with his deep eastern city accent, "Mistaw Ricardo sir. It appears we have a consoyn that gots to be handled."

Ricardo blows out more smoke and looking down into the driver's eyes says, "Oh yeah, what concern you talking about?"

The driver confidently says, "Fawst of all, my employah, Mistah Sawpente, would likes me to tell yaw he don't have any ill feelins towawds you or yaw men. He says that what happened this mawnin is a chance one takes when doing this business. Secondly, he is very pleased to find out that you did make good on yaw end of the bawgain and that it was a full trailaw load just like you promised. Faw that, he would like to commission you to make more faw him."

Ricardo is very happy to hear this. He honestly thought that Mr. Serpente would try to get his money back. He then looks at the driver and says, "Go on."

The driver smiles and says, "You realize he lost a lot of money with this morning's fiasco?"

Ricardo nods his head and says, "Yup."

The driver continues, "He would like to make sure nothins like this happens again. Befaw he pays yaw for this next shipment, which he hopes yaw can have ready faw next Wednesday and which he hopes yaw can have anothaw little somethin in the trailaw too."

Ricardo is excited inside but isn't showing it on the outside asks, "What little something?"

The driver nods his head and points to a couple of bruises on his face, "Yaw see, the lady and haw pawtnaw, needs to be with this shipment. Mistah Sawpente will pay yaw double the amount. If yaw can't delivah both, then he don't want any. They have to be alive."

The excitement is overwhelming Ricardo, but still standing strong inhales very long finishing his cigarette with one breath. After a long exhale and relighting of another he says, "Let me get this straight, if I have Zorra and this other person inside the trailer, alive with the heroin, he will pay me double the amount?"

"That's correct suh." The driver smiles and then asks while extending his hand for a shake, "Do we have ourselves an agreement?"

Ricardo squints his eyes and nods his head very slightly then says, "Not so fast. This Zorra is a major douche. You see, the mayor of this city wants me to get her for him."

The driver looks at his mates and says, "Let's go. Looks like we gots to talks to the mayaw."

Ricardo urgently stops the driver from leaving, "Whoa, whoa, whoa, not so fast. The mayor is off-limits. Only, I, speak to him. I didn't say I wouldn't do this for you. She is just too hard to get."

Mr. Serpente's man says, "She's just a gal. Yaw telling me yaw guys can't get a little gal. I'll let Mistah Sawpente know that yaw awe the wrong men faw the job. He can get someone else to make his smack."

Ricardo snaps his fingers and twenty of his Peligrosa surround Mr. Serpente's men with guns drawn. "Now, gentlemen, we ain't done this conversation, so you ain't going nowhere yet. Apparently according to your face, mister driver, you too couldn't handle a little girl."

The driver looks around him very upset, "Yaw holdin us at gun point. This convawsation is ovaw unless yaw lowaw yaw guns. Besides it wasn't haw who handcuffed me it was the deputy."

A little more intrigued, Ricardo waves his men to back off, which they do. Then he asks, "What do you mean deputy? From what we know she has been working by herself."

The driver answers, "Yeah, that's right a deputy. He pulled me ovaw and took the truck. She then came ovaw and hit me a couple times in the head then took off aftaw him in haw caw."

"Well sir," Ricardo says, "could you be so kind and describe this deputy for me? This is the first I have heard about anyone helping her."

"Wait a sec," the annoyed driver says then continues, "yaws got someone hoytin yaw guys and yaw don't know shes got a pawtnah. I know yaw was a two-bit thug. You aint awganized."

Ricardo, lost his temper and very upset grabs the driver and hoists him up eye-to-eye, "Listen you piece of shit. The Peligrosa has been around for many decades now... we aint two-bit. The only reason you're still alive is that I would like to continue our business relationship with Mr. Serpente. Now, describe this deputy or the four of you won't leave here alive." Again, even more Peligrosa, some with guns, others with bats, chains, and crowbars, surrounded the four men. Ricardo throws the man to the ground standing tall above waiting for an answer.

The driver gets up a little shaken but answers, "Mistah Sawpente will hear about this, yaw know." The driver takes a few seconds to assess the situation and continues, "The deputy was a little too big faw his unifom around the mid section if yaw know what I mean. He's a wetback like yaw and walks with a limp. He knowz how to handle himself. He plays his role just fine."

Ricardo's eyes and grin widens and anxiously says, "You tell Mr. Serpente he's got himself a deal." Ricardo extends his hand.

"Yaw know whos he is?" the driver asks.

"Oh, I know. This is the best news I have heard in a week. Now shake. We got a deal." Ricardo and the driver shake hands. "You guys are free to go. Everything will be ready for Wednesday."

Ricardo's men back off letting Mr. Serpente's men leave. As soon as the door shuts, Ricardo tells one of his henchmen, "Take a few men and follow those guys outside of city limits. I want them to have enough time to talk with Mr. Serpente so he knows the deal is on. Make sure you take the unmarked vehicles. I don't want them to know you're Peligrosa. Kill them. Make sure it looks like Zorra did it."

"How do we do that?"

"I don't know! Shit, slice their foreheads. That's her MO, isn't it? Nobody makes fun of us."

"Yes sir, Ricardo! My pleasure!" His henchman left gathering several of his friends.

Another one of Ricardo's men, an elderly individual, approaches him and asks, "What about tonight? How do you know if Zorra will arrive tonight? Do you want me to have the guys spread word in the alleys?"

Ricardo quickly chirps, "No, I don't want anyone to be warned. I'll be fine if Zorra doesn't show up. We're going to still blow up the entire block so that the mayor thinks she's dead."

The older Peligrosa says, "We need her alive. She's a handful that one. How are we gonna capture her?"

Ricardo smiling says, "I now know her weak spot. Don't you worry, by tomorrow, we will have her and her friend."

"So, you do know who this deputy is? Is it who I think it is?" the old Peligrosa asks.

"Do you know of anyone else in this city that thinks he's untouchable? He thinks I won't harm him. He's right. I won't harm him. I'll just have Mr. Serpente do it." Both Ricardo and the older Peligrosa laugh at the thought.

CHAPTER 21

# HERE COMES THE CROSS

A startling crash of glass and thud catches Alejandro's attention. He quickly jumps out of his recliner. He draws the revolver out of its holster that is snug around his waist and limps towards his bedroom in the direction of the shattering. He hugs the wall in the hallway next to his open bedroom door feeling a breeze. He bends his arm in to turn on the lights. After a few deep breaths he announces, "I have a loaded gun and am an excellent shot. You have to the count of three before I open fire. You should be on the ground face down with your hands on your head if you want to see the sun come up tomorrow. One… two…" Alejandro ducks and gives a shoulder roll into his room ready to fire. All he sees besides a broken window and shards of glass on the floor is a brick with a note tied to it. Alejandro heads to the window and slowly looks out to see if he can catch anyone. No one is in sight. Just smoke coming from the end of a lit cigarette on the ground in his alley.

The brick was tossed perfectly between the bars. Alejandro unties the note from the brick. He opens it up and quietly reads it.

*The Peligrosa will blow up the church tonight at eight.*

Alejandro looking down at the mess in his room and the way he was given the message drops the brick and note and says, "Ricardo, obviously they know I know her. This is clearly a trap." Alejandro heads back into his living room to call the police. He looks at the time and it is seven-thirty. He calls the precinct and asks for Captain Love. He is told that the captain is unavailable. He then tells the dispatcher that he just received a warning that the church is going to be blown up tonight. Feeling that the call was going nowhere he limps downstairs to the phone book.

Alejandro looks up the phone number for La Santa Maria. He dials it and a very scruffy voice is on the other end, "Hello, you've reached God. What can I do for ya?"

Instantly recognizing the scruffy ignorant voice Alejandro says, "Ricardo, what are you doing? Don't you dare blow up that church!"

"Ha ha ha," a chuckling Ricardo continues, "you're always trying to ruin my fun."

"This isn't a joke. You got my attention. What do you want?"

A few seconds of silence goes by. Alejandro can hear Ricardo dragging on a cigarette and then blowing out hard. With calmness answers, "I want her. Not tonight. Tonight, I'm doing something else. But tomorrow would be good. If she shows up tonight, she will end up dead. I want her alive. Bring her to my place tomorrow to surrender or everyone she is trying to protect will end up like this puny little church will be in half an hour."

Alejandro, knowing exactly whom Ricardo is referring to asks, "Who are you talking about?"

No longer calm but still serious Ricardo answers, "Alejandro, this isn't a game. Bring her to me. Not in the morning, I will be celebrating. Bring her to me tomorrow night. I'll be waiting." Then he hangs up.

"He's serious." Alejandro quietly says while he is thinking of what to do next. "This has escalated too far. I can't ask her to help. It's a trap. I'll do it myself."

At La Santa Maria a distraught Father O'Riley is angrily shouting out at Ricardo, "You're mad! There is no mercy for your soul you putrid being!"

Ricardo smiles and then says with an Irish accent, "You are so kind, Father. But flattery won't save you." Ricardo flicks his cigarette at Father O'Riley. He is tied up in his office where Ricardo was awaiting the phone call from Alejandro. The cigarette bounces off his forehead scattering little ash embers. Father O'Riley continues yelling at the intruders. Ricardo points to one of his men and says, "Gag him will you. Let him pray in silence while his church collapses on top of him." Ricardo, then with an evil sneer says to the priest, "The weight of the church will be on your shoulders. Where's your God now? Ha ha ha ha!"

Ricardo leaves the office and heads towards the gold cross yelling out, "It's showtime everyone! While our buddies are keeping the good cops busy on the other side of the city, we have this church all to ourselves." He lights up another cigarette and continues announcing while several of the Peligrosa are attaching a harness to the cross. "Alejandro should be here soon. That limp of his might slow him down. Keep your eyes out for Zorra! She and Alejandro need to be taken alive. The helicopter should be here anytime. This is important Peligrosa!" Ricardo speaks up louder, "Nothing can go wrong! Once the helicopter takes the cross everyone get out of here. I'm heading to the mayor's penthouse now. The moment I see the gold on the mayor's balcony I will be detonating the dynamite in the van. So, when you scatter out of here, I want to remind everyone not to take the van. Does everyone understand?"

A score of Peligrosa, men, and women, yell out to Ricardo letting him know they understand. The adrenaline is pumping hard through their veins. Ricardo checks the harness and warns William, his number one man, that he is counting on him for everything to move smoothly. He also reminds him to be vigilant and to keep his eye out for Alejandro and Zorra. It's of the utmost importance that they are to capture them alive. The money they will be making from selling Alejandro and Zorra to Mr. Serpente along with the new heroin production will finally help Ricardo establish his dominance over Perilous City.

As Ricardo walks down the granite steps in front of the church he hears a helicopter approaching. "Good, good," Ricardo confidently says. He then points at William and alerts him, "That's got to be it coming. Here's the flashlight." Ricardo hands him the light. "When he lowers the cable make sure you connect it securely to the cross. Once you flash that light up to the helicopter, the cross will be pulled right out of here. Be clear of the door."

William complies with, "Yes, sir."

Ricardo pats him on the shoulder and leaves him behind. Ricardo ditches his lit cigarette on the ground as he approaches a van parked in front of the church's steps. He swings the back door open and smiles greatly at the amount of dynamite stacked in the van. He reaches in and flips a switch to turn on the remote receiver. Ricardo makes sure he puts his remote detonator into his leather vest pocket. After he closes the door, he lights another cigarette and heads to the car ready to take him to the mayor's townhouse.

Unaware of peeping eyes, Ricardo doesn't notice a small stealthy figure watching from across the road, hiding in the dark shadows of a doorway behind a covered bus stop waiting area. A fully clothed and refreshed Zorra holds back from darting over. As much as she would like to remove Ricardo from this world, Zorra notices the large number of Peligrosa hanging outside the church. She watches Ricardo climb into a car and drive away. Zorra was about to leave her hiding spot when a taxi pulled up on her side of the six-lane road. She sees Alejandro get out of the taxi right in front of the bus stop. At the same time, she sees a helicopter appearing through the smog right above the church. As the taxi drives away Zorra jogs down the stairs and pulls Alejandro behind the bus stop.

"Josefina, what are you doing here?" a startled Alejandro asks.

Speaking over the noise of the helicopter but still out of view of the Peligrosa, Zorra responds, "I was getting myself ready for a night stroll when I heard a helicopter fly over. I followed it here. It's been circling the church for a while. What are you doing here?"

Alejandro answers, "It's not safe here. Ricardo is going to blow the church up. You got to go. I must stop Ricardo."

A puzzled Zorra replies, "Ricardo's not here. He just left. He left moments before you arrived."

Admiring Zorra's attention to detail and her proven past surveillance, Alejandro is very wise when he asks, "What else did you see?"

"There's about two dozen heavily armed Peligrosa here. They're avoiding that van," Zorra points to the van parked directly across from them and continues, "Ricardo didn't even smoke near it. There's something up, I think it might have some explosives in it."

Alejandro turns towards Zorra and holds her shoulders looking her deep into her haunting animal eyes, "Now, I'm not joking. Your instincts are good. Ricardo plans on blowing up the church—"

Zorra interrupts, "I have to save Father O'Riley"

Alejandro abruptly buts in, "Hold on, if that van is rigged to blow, we need to get it out of here."

A puzzled Zorra then asks, "Wait a second, if he plans on blowing up the church, then why is the gold cross still in there." She motions with her head across the road where the church's wooden doors are swung open. The wind is picking up which is quite a very rare occurrence in this muggy metropolis. Zorra then looks at Alejandro, "Wind, this isn't normal wind. That's the helicopter." Both of them look across the road again and notice the helicopter with a cable dragging on the ground. "That's it! They're going to fly the cross out. We have to stop them! Ricardo put what looked like a remote control into his vest. He took it from the van. He won't blow it until he sees the cross wherever it is going. I put my money on the mayor."

Alejandro gives a quick wink, "I can't argue with that one. While they're busy with the cable, let's get a closer look at the back of that van." Alejandro grabs Zorra's hand and they run to the van. He swings the back doors open and they see the van's cargo space is packed with explosives. "There IS enough in here to take down an entire block."

Zorra slyishly smiles, "You know, the mayor's penthouse takes up an entire block."

Alejandro ponders a bit and then looks at Zorra. He is about to agree with her then looks at the van, "No, it can't be that easy." He is now pointing at an on/off toggle switch. He then flicks it off, "There... the red light is out. It's now deactivated."

"Great!" Zorra exclaims, "I've heard the mayor's penthouse is the only residential living space in that building. He's the only one who lives there. The rest of the building is used for businesses. All businesses are closed until tomorrow because of the tunnel explosion."

Alejandro, nodding his head in agreement affirms what she just said, "You are right, Zorra."

Zorra coyishly grins and asserts, "If you take the van and park it in the parking garage…"

Alejandro shook his head in pure defiance, "No Zorra it's too risky. That van needs to leave the city. I've dealt with my fair share of explosions recently."

While they're arguing about what to do with the explosives the two didn't realize the cable had been securely connected to the cross. By the time they catch on the Peligrosa are scrambling out of the building as fast as they can go. Zorra looks over and sees the last remaining Peligrosa flash a light up to the helicopter and dart toward a car. The pilot begins his slow ascent. Zorra gives

Alejandro a big kiss on his cheek and says, "We all have to die sometime." She then gets to her feet and runs up the stairs.

Before Alejandro realizes what is going on, Zorra climbs on top of the cross and is airlifted heading off to her next destination. Alejandro shakes his head in bewilderment, "That brave little soul." He then sees the direction the cross is slowly rising and heading towards… right to the center of the city. "She must be correct, One Bigler Avenue." Alejandro shuts the van door and is confronted by half a dozen Peligrosa with guns drawn.

One of them yells, "Get him quick, Ricardo wants him unharmed!"

Alejandro shouts back, "I guess you don't plan on shooting then. You know, with all this dynamite behind me."

"Everybody put your guns away." The Peligrosa ordered. As soon as they holstered their guns Alejandro un-holsters his Smith & Wesson and with six quick shots all six of their shooting arms are shot out at the elbows.

## CHAPTER 22

# FROM A DIFFERENT POINT OF VIEW

**Point of view: The Good**

After disarming the Peligrosa with six swift shots, Alejandro hobbles to the driver's side of the van and climbs in. He cautiously drives off towards the penthouse. The traffic is almost nonexistent on the way to One Bigler Avenue. Alejandro's main concern is the welfare of the young lady he has hidden from society and has unknowingly given the opportunity to be the greater good in Perilous City. He pulls up to the garage where the attendant notices the Peligrosa van and opens the parking garage door immediately. Just as Zorra had stated, the parking lot was empty excluding Ricardo's ride and the mayor's limousine.

Alejandro parks the van a few car lengths away from the parking garage's elevator. As he climbs out of the van, Alejandro sees a full package of large zip-ties. He says while shoving the package into his back pocket, "This must be one of the vans they use for kidnapping." He opens the back and is about to turn on the remote switch to the explosives but the thought of Zorra being on top of the building stops him from doing it. He says, "Oh, how I wish I knew what was going on up there. I hope she held on tight."

Alejandro limps to the elevator and impatiently presses the elevator's 'up' button several times. He is now waiting for the elevator to come down. "I hope the penthouse doesn't require a special key."

An eternity passes while he watches the numbers tick down. His anxiety is on Zorra's wellbeing. Alejandro checks his handgun to make sure it's fully loaded. He adds six more rounds of the seven rounds of his model 386 Smith & Wesson 357 revolver. He keeps it ready with the safety off. The elevator comes to a stop and the door opens.

An unaware young nose-picking Peligrosa is looking dumbfounded down the barrel of Alejandro's 357's titanium cylinder. Alejandro pushes him back as he enters the elevator, "Get down!" with authority, Alejandro orders, "Face on the ground! Hands on your head!"

The juvenile delinquent does what he is told and then says as the elevator door closes, "But I need to get the handcart. If I don't Ricardo will be mad."

A smile comes to Alejandro's face, "Good, I'm at the right place. Don't worry. If everything works out, you won't be needing the handcart. How many of you are up there?" Alejandro asks as he zip-ties the thug's legs and arms. He then pushes the penthouse button.

The elevator starts to climb when the young man nervously speaks up when he answers, "Four of us, well five if you count the mayor."

A relieved Alejandro says, "Oh good, you're out of the picture and the mayor is useless, Ricardo will cower to me. Like he always has. It only leaves two. I like these odds."

*A Legend Awakens*

The hoodlum then says, "Ricardo's got plans for you and Zorra. He will do anything he can to stop you."

As the elevator heads for its destination, Alejandro lectures the boy, "Now, young man, don't waste your time emulating a no-good thug like Ricardo. His future is set. He is a waste. You, however, have a chance to turn yourself around. You can't be older than eighteen. Drugs and death await you now. Overcome it. Become somebody. This city will need good kids with strong minds to clean up the garbage. You can be one of those—"

"Shut up old man! As soon as this door opens, I'm warning them."

Alejandro now saddened shakes his head in disappointment, "How I wish you would have been one of the ones with a strong mind." Alejandro rips the young man's shirt off and gags him silent.

The elevator makes it to the penthouse and the door opens. Alejandro looks out and sees no one there. Directly across the hallway is the entrance to the mayor's office. He can hear someone yelling and the whomping sound of the helicopter's propeller. Alejandro presses the 'stop' button keeping the elevator doors open. He then stands his captive up and zip-ties him to the railing inside the elevator.

Alejandro opens the door to the penthouse's office. He sees off in the distance on the open balcony an irate-acting Ricardo and his two henchmen looking up into the sky. Just thirty feet away at his desk with the chair facing the window, Mayor Bigler is screaming into his phone yelling directions to his nephew who is piloting the helicopter. Alejandro approaches the mayor and points the gun at his temple.

Mayor Bigler turns his head slowly to see Alejandro pointing a gun in his face, "You almost got it. I've got to go for now." The mayor hangs up his phone and then asks, "Who in hell are you?"

Alejandro reaching for the mayor's arm says, "Never mind who I am, Mayor, you're coming with me. Quietly I hope."

The mayor pulls his shoulder away from him, "I don't want any trouble. Are you the FBI? I can't go now. I am expecting two important items. One should be dropping in any moment now."

"Fine then," Alejandro grabs some more zip-ties from his back pocket and straps the mayor into his chair, "you're coming with me." Alejandro rolls the mayor out of his office and into the elevator where the young wide-eyed Peligrosa is standing. Alejandro says to his captives, "Keep each other company." As Alejandro is zip-tying the mayor's chair to the rail in the elevator an extremely loud uproar occurs. The penthouse shakes a bit with a loud thunderous crash. Then a continuous collision of a crashing commotion keeps occurring but slowly gets quieter. Alejandro quickly skips and hobbles into the office and along with two Peligrosa and Ricardo, is mesmerized by a large gaping hole in the ceiling and in the floor.

**Point of view: The Brave**

Back when the cross had just started taking off into the smog the nervous Zorra says, "What in hell am I doing? Josefina, you have surely taken on something you can't handle." Zorra is straddling the top of the cross holding the cable as tight as she can. The helicopter is slowly raising the heavy spinning cross through the cloud of smog. A familiar cold chill is taking over her body just like when she was on top of the canyon walls the other night. Zorra orders herself, "Think think, think!"

Zorra is once again amazed by the tremendous view of the night sky when the cross arises above the smog. The winds are whipping hard but the smog only swirls at the top being stopped by Mayor Bigler's penthouse. Zorra reaches into her backpack and pulls out a small hacksaw, "This should do the trick." She starts to saw at the cable. "Wait a second. If this cable breaks the cross will fall and this cable will snap back sending me flying." Zorra puts the hacksaw back into her backpack and commences to climb up the cable. By the time the helicopter makes it to its destination, Zorra completes her climb.

Braving the cold wind Zorra starts to saw at the cable wrapped around a landing skid. The pilot has no clue what is going on. He looks down at the penthouse and sees Ricardo and a couple of Peligrosa waving his arms and pointing up at him. The pilot waves down to them all excited thinking they're happy to see him. His cell phone starts buzzing. His flying helmet is synced to it via Bluetooth, "Hello."

Sitting on the chair behind his penthouse's office desk, Mayor John Bigler is looking out of his window talking to his nephew, "What a great boy you are. Not only did you bring me my gold, but you also have my Zorra hanging on for dear life. This is what I mean by if you want something done right you need family to do it."

The confused pilot asks his uncle, "Do you want me to shake her off?"

The mayor quickly answers, "No, no, no don't shake her off. Well actually, that's a good idea. The fall to the ground would surely crush everything. I want her head in perfect condition. Fly above the building and shake her off on top. The fall should kill her and the porch should catch her." His nephew raises the helicopter another couple hundred feet above the penthouse. He starts wobbling and spinning the helicopter. While the mayor watches a gun is pointed at his temple. Mayor Bigler turns his head slowly to see Alejandro pointing a gun in his face. The mayor says to his nephew, "You almost got it. I've got to go for now."

His nephew answers, "Okie dokie! Over and out." Zorra has her legs wrapped tightly around the landing skid and continues to rapidly hack away at the cable. She is trying her best to release the cross. Now since she sees a beautiful target below, her willpower has increased. She sees Ricardo on the porch pressing his remote and then throwing it off the building. She thinks to herself, *Apparently, Alejandro didn't turn the bomb on. Poor Ricardo, his plan has been foiled. No explosion today.*

The pilot is doing a great job. During one of his spins and a quick jerk, Zorra almost slips off. She must hug the skid with her other arm and the hacksaw falls. After stabilizing her leg grip, Zorra reaches into her bag again not willing to give up. She pulls out a flashlight, looks at it with disgust, thinking *where were you last night*, then gives it a heave-ho. She reaches into her bag another time and pulls out some duct tape. That too is about to get tossed until she quickly thinks of a way she can use it. She loosens the end with her teeth then wraps the tape around her legs keeping herself pinned to the landing skid. She also tapes her left hand to the landing skid. She is not worried about falling off now. She has one more item in her backpack that she knows should finish the job.

Blindly feeling around and after another jostle from the pilot, "Eureka!" she exclaims! Now she is looking at one of the many guns she has taken from the Peligrosa. She points it right at the spot she has been diligently sawing and pulls the trigger. BANG!!! SNAP!!!! The gun falls from her grip. While spinning she watches the gun fall further and further away just as she watches the ½ ton cross of solid gold disappear into the roof.

With the loss of the heavy cargo, the helicopter quickly raises another couple hundred feet where the pilot finally stops shaking and spinning. He flips on the searchlight and lowers the helicopter about fifty feet above the hole in the roof. The light lit up a very, very deep hole. Within seconds a strange wave vibration flexes through the building sending a shockwave to the helicopter. A flash of flames shoots through the hole frightening the pilot. He quickly turns the helicopter around and heads to return it to the police station. The helicopter disappears into the smog.

## Point of view: The Dumb

While the helicopter is rising through the smog to deliver the large gold cross, Ricardo and his Peligrosa thugs arrive at One Bigler Avenue. The security guard gives them immediate access to the vacant garage. The driver parks next to the mayor's limousine.

Ricardo says to his men, "Okay guys, let's get up there and get this done. The sooner we get this done, the sooner we can collect our reward for the cross." He inserts his key and presses the button for the penthouse. While the elevator begins its ascent, Ricardo checks his phone, "No messages about Alejandro or Zorra. I thought for sure one of them would have shown up. We better see them tomorrow."

"What if they don't show up, Ricardo?" one of his men asks.

Ricardo shrugs it off then says, "He will. He has to."

Then the other Peligrosa speculates, "Yeah, but what if she doesn't show up and our guys don't catch her? And then you blow up the block. Your plan is to tell the mayor she was a part of that explosion, right?"

A reassured Ricardo answers, "Don't worry about the little things boys. I've got it all taken care of. He'll show up and so won't she. It's in their nature. By tomorrow night I'll have them both."

The other Peligrosa who is feeding off the other one's vibe, "But, the mayor wants her head. What if she doesn't show, the block blows, you tell him she's dead and then she shows back up alive?"

Becoming annoyed, the fearless Ricardo answers, "After the block blows and that pesky church is destroyed, Alejandro will have no choice but to bring her. The mayor is so out of the loop, I will give him the head of some other woman. He'll have no clue." Ricardo looks at the elevator's floor display ticking away then warns, "No more talking about this. Oh, and grab as much gold trinkets as you can. Just don't get caught."

The elevator makes it to its destination. When the elevator doors open, a happy mayor welcomes them into his penthouse with open arms, "Come in come in. My nephew should be here any moment with my cross. He picked it up about a minute ago. Would you like some drinks?" Before anyone answers, the giddy mayor pours them all moldy screwdrivers.

Ricardo and his men gladly accept their drinks. Ricardo enjoys the little twist from the original screwdriver by adding blue curaçao to it. He drinks it down immediately and holding the empty glass towards the mayor he looks for another. The only response is the mayor ignoring his request. Ricardo then puts his hand in his pocket feeling the remote detonator getting anxious to see the helicopter with its golden contraband so he can press the button.

The other Peligrosa downed their drinks as quickly as Ricardo had. The entourage walks behind the mayor through his home office pocketing gold trinkets here and there. The mayor shows them the location where they will bring the cross. Its new resting place will be the large empty spot right next to the cabinet with Joaquin Murrieta's head.

The mayor sighs a bit when looking at the cabinet then reminds Ricardo, "Don't forget I would really enjoy seeing that she-devil, Zorra's head right next to Zorro's."

Ricardo tells the mayor, "Yes, mayor, I'm awaiting news anytime now about her capture. If everything goes smoothly you'll have her head soon."

The mayor childishly claps and then asks in remembrance, "Did your guys tell the alley dwellers that we are to blow up the church in hopes Zorra would find out?"

With assurance, Ricardo replies, "My guys were all over it." The other Peligrosa with him chuckles a bit knowing that Zorra is going to a higher bidder.

The mayor points in the direction of the balcony and excitedly announces, "Oh great look there it is." Off in a distance, the helicopter lifts itself and the cross out of the smog and is now high above the filthy city below. The mayor says with a tear running from his eye, "Isn't she gorgeous."

"Come on guys, let's get this done." Ricardo points to one of his men, "You, bring the handcart."

The Peligrosa he just pointed to asks, "What handcart?"

The other Peligrosa says, "The one in the trunk of the car."

Ricardo shakes his head in bewilderment and looks around at all of them, "You dumb-asses. Go get the god-damn handcart." He tosses the younger Peligrosa the key to the elevator.

"Will do boss." He says as he makes his way to the elevator.

"Good help I got, smart help I don't." Ricardo mutters quietly as he heads for the balcony.

The mayor points to the helicopter and yells out to Ricardo, "Why is one doohickey bigger than the other?"

Ricardo squints his eyes and quietly expresses, "What doohickey? God, he's stupid." He then studies the helicopter a bit more.

Panicking, one of the Peligrosa says, "That, that's Zorra. Oh, shit."

"No it can't be," Ricardo hesitantly says. After another few moments of concentrating on the skids he then nervously says, "Oh shit! It's her. And she's cutting the cable!" Ricardo opens the balcony door and runs out there. He starts waving and pointing at her on the helicopter trying to get the pilot's attention. He then yells at the Peligrosa, "Tell the mayor it's Zorra and she is trying to cut the cable! He needs to warn his nephew!"

The mayor gets on his phone instantly and calls him. His nephew answers the phone, "Hello."

The mayor rocks back in his chair with his eyes glued on the hypnotizing pendulum action of the golden cross swaying several hundred feet or so along the side of his building. He then tells his nephew, "What a great boy you are. Not only did you bring me my gold, you also have my Zorra hanging on for dear life. This is what I mean by if you want something done right you need family to do it."

The confused pilot asks his uncle, "Do you want me to shake her off?"

The mayor quickly answers, "No, no, no don't shake her off. Well, actually that's a good idea. The fall to the ground would surely crush everything. I want her head in perfect condition. Fly above the building and shake her off on top. The fall should kill her and the porch should catch her. You almost got it. I've got to go for now."

"Okie dokie! Over and out," his nephew promptly replies and raises the helicopter a couple hundred feet above the penthouse.

Ricardo and his two goons watch as the pilot starts rocking and spinning the helicopter. One of them says, "What's he trying to do, get her sick?"

"No, you idiot. He's trying to knock her off." Ricardo rolls his eyes and lights another cigarette. As he puts his lighter away, he remembers about the explosives. "That's right…," Ricardo grabs the remote. He then announces to the other two, "Ready gentlemen? Look over there." He says while pointing off in the distance and continues talking, "That's where the church is. We should be able to see the explosion through the smog." Ricardo presses the button.

The big grin on Ricardo's face goes south as one of the Peligrosa says to him, "Did you press it? I didn't see nothin."

Ricardo presses it several times. Each time a little harder and with less patience. Besides the regular swirl marks of the wind trying to break through the smog, there was nothing. No movement or flash of light. Ricardo starts swearing up a storm and launches the remote off the building. He then grabbed his cell phone to see if there were any messages… still none. Ricardo dials his 'number one' and waits for an answer. The phone goes right into voice messaging. Ricardo yells into it, "Yeah I'll leave a fucking message! Zorra is here and no explosion! You better have Alejandro."

Ricardo starts pacing now worrying about Zorra's head going to the mayor and losing out on his money. He gets interrupted in his thought and jumps back when a hacksaw crashes onto the balcony. He looks up towards the helicopter thinking it was Zorra. As he looks up, he sees a flashlight falling just missing the building. He then says, "She should be falling soon."

The other Peligrosa says, "Looks like she is taping herself to the chopper."

"She ain't fallin off then," Ricardo asserts, "After we get this cross loaded onto the cart, we need to get to that police station pronto. She'll be landing there."

"Speaking of the handcart, where is that kid?" a Peligrosa asked. "He should be back now with that thing."

Ricardo, more worried about getting Zorra alive than the cross says, "You guys can handle this. I'm heading to the station now."

"Looks like she's done taping herself, Ricardo, and she's reaching in her bag again." One of the henchmen says while pointing up. The helicopter is still swaying back and forth trying to knock Zorra off. The pilot has no clue she has taped herself securely. Then the henchman asks, "Is that a gun?"

Ricardo stops in his tracks and looks up. He sees a muzzle flash. Ricardo yells out, "Shit! Duck and cover!" Ricardo and his men jump towards the edge of the balcony and an extremely loud uproar occurs. The penthouse shakes a bit with a loud crash. Then a continuous collision of a crashing commotion keeps occurring but slowly gets quieter.

Ricardo scrambles to his feet and runs into the office. His two cronies follow suit. While standing mesmerized by a large gaping hole in the ceiling and in the floor, Alejandro hobbles into the room.

Standing on opposite sides of the room, Alejandro's and Ricardo's eyes meet. The two Peligrosa carefully bend over the hole in the floor to see the damage. A large shockwave flows through the four men. Then a large flame blasts through, burning the faces off the two Peligrosa. The power turns off in the penthouse and the whole building starts trembling.

The two burnt Peligrosa are screaming in agony when Alejandro speaks out, "Calm down, this building is collapsing."

Ricardo asks, "What, why is this building collapsing?" Another tremor shakes the building again. Mayor Bigler's emergency electric backup turns on. The two badly burned Peligrosa are tugging Ricardo for help.

Alejandro answers, "Your van of explosives was in the garage, right about where the hole is."

The Peligrosa's moans of pain become too annoying for Ricardo. He pulls his gun out and shoots both of them right in their heads. The building starts trembling uncontrollably. Ricardo replies, "You bastard, you brought the van here. Now we're both dead."

Shocked at what he just witnessed, Alejandro says, "They needed medical attention."

Ricardo not giving a shit says, "Screw you, they are out of pain now." Ricardo and Alejandro are standing with their guns drawn. The tremors of the building start to get worse. Ricardo lowers his gun, "I'm not gonna kill you. I promised Angela I wouldn't." He puts his gun away and yells, "Where's that asshole mayor?" Ricardo points to the hole.

Alejandro shakes his head, "No, no, he's in the elevator." Ricardo heads for the elevator with Alejandro following, "Ricardo, what caused the hole?" Alejandro knows it could only be one thing. He just hopes Zorra jumped off. He asks again, "Was it the cross? Was she on it?"

Ricardo turns and sneers, "The cable broke… your Zorra went down with it."

A large pain of loss instantly fills Alejandro's heart. He stumbles on his way to the elevator and rests against the wall. Ricardo sees his henchman and the mayor zip-tied to the elevator.

Ricardo notices Alejandro sitting on the floor propped against the wall pale and in tears. Ricardo then turns and looks at the mayor and gives a great big grin. The puppy-eyed mayor asks Ricardo, "Did my gold make it safely?"

The tremors in the building are now continuous. Ricardo cuts the mayor loose when he says, "Yeah, it's in your office." The mayor gets up and passes Alejandro and darts into his office. Ricardo yells to Alejandro, "What's your plan? You gonna die in a collapsing building without dignity? I'm gonna take this elevator down a few floors and see if I can make a jump to the next building."

The mayor comes back into the hallway and loses his composure, "Ricardo, there is a large hole where my gold should be! What is going on?" he demanded.

Ricardo leaves the elevator and grabs Alejandro by his arm. While dragging him into the elevator he answers the mayor, "You fuckin idiot, it's in the parking garage." Ricardo presses the start button to reactivate the elevator door. With the elevator back on, Ricardo cuts the other Peligrosa free and throws him out of the elevator. The ejected Peligrosa knocks the mayor back. Ricardo presses the close button and with a vindictive smile waves goodbye to the mayor. Ricardo chooses a floor thirty stories below hoping it will bring him closer to another building. As it starts going down, he looks down at Alejandro. He shakes his head, "I should have left you there. I won't be able to carry your ass over to the next building."

Alejandro raises his head and looks into Ricardo's eyes, "Why did you save me? At Mama's funeral, you made it clear you couldn't wait to watch me die."

"If I left you up there, I wouldn't see you die. I also told Angela I wouldn't kill you." At this moment the supporting structures on the lower floors could sustain no more weight and the building collapses floor by floor. A large cloud of debris and dust pillows through the air as One Bigler Avenue is reduced to a pile of rubble.

CHAPTER 23

# A Great Loss

"**WAIT! WAIT! WHAT JUST HAPPENED! TAKE ME BACK!**" Zorra is yelling to the helicopter at the top of her vocal range. She knows the explosion only means one thing; Alejandro got the truck back to One Bigler Avenue. As the helicopter continues its descent through the smog, Zorra shifts her thoughts from Alejandro, who she hopes dropped the explosives off and escaped unscathed, to dismounting the helicopter's landing skid.

Pinned tightly to the landing skid, Zorra gets a great view of the Police Station's helicopter pad. *Shit*, she thinks to herself as she sees the landing pad get larger, worried the police will be ready to snatch her. No one is present at the top of the station. *It makes sense; they're probably all heading to the mayor's building.* She starts removing the tape from around her left arm and hurriedly removes the tape from her legs as the helicopter comes to a safe landing. With now being several stories above the ground the massive cloud of deconstruction dust and smoke billowing from One Bigler Avenue added to the regular thick air pollution keeps it in suspension longer than it should. The horrible air has nowhere to go and easily takes over the entire city. The visibility is nil.

Zorra intently watches for the pilot to leave the helicopter. She makes out his silhouette and watches him rush into the stairwell on the roof. She decides to take refuge inside the helicopter instead of following him into a building potentially filled with police. The air quality is much better inside the cockpit, but she knows it is a temporary fix.

Even though the police station is further away from One Bigler Avenue than from Josefina's and Alejandro's Diner, the chaotic aftermath of debris is pillowing very thick. The emergency vehicles heading for the collapsed building and security alarms are echoing throughout the city. Just like the citizens of New York City after the World Trade Center terrorist attack of 2001, the citizens of Perilous City need to stay indoors and cover their mouths so they don't inhale the soot. Unlike the collapse of the World Trade Center, the destructive repercussion won't be as severe since the explosion brought the building down from the foundation. The large hole that went up the entire building made it crumble inward.

The next two hours felt like a hundred years for Zorra. Anxious to get out of the helicopter and to get away from the police station, Zorra is curious to see if she can escape without suffocating on the falling cloud of soot. She opens the helicopter door to gauge the debris. In contradiction to the dust of the wreckage everywhere, the visibility of the air is remarkably better. Besides worrying about the safety of Alejandro, Zorra was also concerned about the welfare of the homeless in the immediate vicinity. She was so anxious earlier hoping the bomb would destroy the building, that she neglected the potential destructive aftermath. Two hours, how can the visibility be this good?

How can the collapse of the tallest building in the city, a symbol of tyranny and suppression, virtually unpopulated at the time, cause any more mayhem and possibly heartache in a city that has had so much internal turmoil for years? It doesn't. The pure destruction and chaos from the aftermath become a catalyst for a larger and

*A Legend Awakens*

well-needed positive event. Just like pulling the drain plug from a full bathtub, One Bigler Avenue being torn down from the sky opened a funnel of air that was once impeded by its unnatural presence. The air currents that were blocked by the building causing the air pollution to maintain in a constant suspension above the city started drifting away down the valley. The billowing debris settled down quicker than expected.

Zorra makes a very important decision. Knowing the area around the destroyed building is loaded with all the city's paramedics, firefighters, and police officers, she decides to head back to Alejandro's. The commute to the restaurant isn't slowed. She was expecting a bit of looting assuming the residents would be taking advantage of the chaos. If the residents aren't sleeping, then they're watching the news or have already gone to the disaster scene to help. With only a few hours left until sunrise Zorra makes it to the restaurant to find it completely barren of life. She sees his broken bedroom window. She carefully climbs the dumpster, makes it to the ledge, and climbs through the window successfully not cutting herself. She calls out for Alejandro.

Zorra slowly investigates his room and turns the light on. Instantly she notices shards of glass all over the floor. She sees the brick and a piece of paper amongst the glass fragments. Quickly picking up the note she whispers, "The Peligrosa will blow up the church tonight at eight." She heads downstairs and Alejandro is nowhere to be found.

A little puzzled and concerned, hoping for the best but assuming the worst, Zorra looks over the mess in the room once more and reads the note to herself, "THEY KNOW," she exclaims! "They figured out Alejandro would go to the church. They wanted him so they could get to me. He had to be the only one to drive the van to the mayor's." Zorra drops the note and heads downstairs still talking to herself, "One of two things, he was in the building, or he left the van and headed here or to my apartment."

Zorra rushes out of the restaurant and heads back to her apartment cutting through the alleyways. Nothing and no one stopped her from running to her apartment in record time. Alejandro's absence from his restaurant mirrored his absence from her apartment. Zorra sees herself in the mirror and sees her disguise is filthy from all the debris resembling a faded version of her clean costume. Still thinking of the broken window and note left in Alejandro's apartment, Zorra changes into a cleaner costume. She is in complete denial of Alejandro's possible death. Zorra, while reapplying her makeup, confidently looks into her reflection in the mirror and says, "The Peligrosa, they captured him. They brought him to the railyard. That must be it. He's not here. He better be at the railyard. They want me, they can have me. I got to get there, fast!"

The quickest way for Zorra to commute to the Peligrosa's hideout is down in the apartment's garage. The revving of the 350 Z's engine brings forth a familiar reverberation of the distinct sound emitting from the garage. The power door opens and Zorra rockets out of the garage in such a fashion she leaves the door open not looking back. The lack of traffic makes it much easier for her to enjoy the actual ride of her new favorite set of wheels. She pulls into the railyard without a plan. She stops with the Peligrosa's building off in the distance wanting to gather some form of preparation. Zorra grabs the binoculars behind the passenger seat. She scans every window carefully and sees no one. While she is sitting there surveying, Zorra thinks back to the times Alejandro supplied her with weapons and gear. She realizes with her hastened departure she has none of her things with her. She smiles and says, "Alejandro has not let me down yet." She jumps out of the Z and opens the very small trunk. Inside it are several handguns, brass knuckles, more asps, a very sharp thicker short sword with a proper sheath. Zorra straps the short sword to her waist already liking the solid feel. She slides one of the brass knuckles on her right hand. She leaves the Z behind to sneak into the building.

Based on an outside reconnaissance there is nobody standing guard of the building. Zorra climbs to a second-story window. She pushes it open to investigate. She is now in the filthiest bathroom she has ever seen. Zorra leaves the bathroom and enters the living quarters where a handful of women and men Peligrosa are passed out from drinking and drugs. Zorra zips past them unconcerned with their useless souls. She moves stealthily out of the room and heads down the hallway where she can hear some nervous banter from downstairs. Zorra is a little thrown back when she sees some gaudy tulip wallpaper going the extent of the hallway and down the stairwell. As she tiptoes through the tulips, down the stairsteps, she sees a man of small stature, on the last stair with bad posture.

Zorra comes up behind him, removes his handgun, and quietly asks with the gun to his back, "You must be Tiny Tim?"

The startled Peligrosa jumps around and says, "No, I'm William."

Zorra inquisitively studies him up and down, "I know you," Zorra says looking at the man who has one eye covered with an eye patch. She notices how nervous he is. She then asks while pointing the gun to his eye patch, "I did that, didn't I? At the church, I shoved my asp in your eye?"

William slowly backs up and stammers, "y-y-y-yes."

She slowly walks with him and says, "I would love to tell you, 'I'm sorry,' but I'm not."

The chatter on the main floor in the warehouse has stopped. Zorra and William look and notice an audience of a couple of dozen shocked Peligrosa looking back at them. *Oh crap*, Zorra scarily thinks, *the element of surprise is gone.* She looks back at William as he grabs the gun. The two start wrestling it back and forth. Tired of the tug o' war, Zorra maintains a tight grip with her left on the gun and sharply throws a skull cracking right, dead center into William's forehead leaving an imprinted bloody "ZORRA" with her brass knuckles. She smiles and thinks, *nice touch Alejandro.*

William lets go of the gun and stumbles back a bit. He feels the pool of blood at the spot where his Peligrosa tattoo is. Well, now was. William, disfigured twice by Zorra, looks at her with a fox-pelt-red blur quickly approaching his head. Zorra follows her punch with a round-kick to the side of William's head sending him directly to the ground.

One of the Peligrosa in the pack yells to the others who were just moments earlier having a nervous discussion about the chaos in the city, "That's Zorra, she's here! Remember, Ricardo wants her!" Zorra smiles hearing Ricardo's name, knowing what she saw only a few hours earlier. Happy with the demise of Ricardo, she turns towards the crowd, in which half of them have guns drawn. The same Peligrosa continues, "We need her alive!"

As the Peligrosa approached her, Zorra put out her arms as if in a surrender position and demanded, "Tell me where he is and I promise you you'll die quickly."

Another Peligrosa looks perturbed and she boldly announces, "You, you're the small thing that has been taking out our guys? You come to our home and think you're in control!"

Ignoring her statement, Zorra asks, "Where is he?"

"He who, Ricardo? He's not here yet."

"No, not Ricardo, he went down with the mayor's building. I want Alejandro. Where are you keeping him?"

Another Peligrosa says, "Where have you been? The city is all fucked up. We don't know where anyone is. Honey, we're on a need-to-know basis. The only one here who knows what is going on is William. And you fucked him up."

A second Peligrosa pointed out, "Well, if Ricardo went down with the building, then I guess we don't need her alive anymore."

Zorra, who is always paying attention to her surroundings, has already located several spots where she can take cover in this heroin lab if it is required. She has already counted twenty-four Peligrosa of which half have guns and the others are just hanging out. Then she says in a similar fashion, "Well, if William is the only one who knows anything then what do I need any of you for?"

Zorra unsheathes her short sword and slashes at a couple of Peligrosa slicing their necks and rolls to safety behind a cabinet in the area where the heroin is made. She points the gun over the cabinet and unloads all the bullets towards the warehouse where the twenty-two standing Peligrosa scatter. Zorra, not liking the gun, runs out from her cover. She tosses the gun in the direction of her next target. As the startled Peligrosa tries to catch the gun, Zorra's blade flows swiftly into his chest.

A startled Peligrosa yells out, "Stop her!" A hail of gunfire commences. Zorra swings the Peligrosa she has impaled to block some of the flying bullets. She then jumps back to the stairwell and runs up. She runs by the passed-out Peligrosa and goes out the window which she entered earlier. Her crazy plan is to head to the door on the loading dock at the back of the building where she got her brother's bike back from Ricardo.

A couple Peligrosa hesitantly followed her up. They yelled down to the others, "She's gone! She came in through the bathroom window! She's gone! Go get her!" A few of the Peligrosa scamper to the door.

As Zorra makes it to the loading dock the door swings open. Zorra pounces hard and starts hacking. One of the Peligrosa yells out, "The zorra is back!"

After a scene worthy of the Coliseum in ancient Rome, Zorra is once again in the warehouse with a pile of Peligrosa at her feet. She announces to the remaining Peligrosa, "That takes care of the guns." Zorra puts the sword back in its sheath. She picks up a gun and points it at the rest of them. She leads the remaining unarmed Peligrosa and the ones who were still alive but heavily bleeding from the onslaught, further into the heroin lab. "There, plenty of tape." She has a couple of them tape their arms and legs behind their backs with the tape. Zorra then finishes the taping of the last one.

*JH Mull*

"You're probably wondering what is going on. Well years ago, the Peligrosa killed off my family and burnt my home down." She grabs the medallion around her neck. "This is all that I have left. Everything you have will be gone now." Zorra grabs all the flammable materials from the lab and buries the live Peligrosa in pallets, crates, rags, and boxes. She goes to the side of the warehouse with their vehicles. They have their gas pump there. She tapes the handle so that the gas continuously pours out of the pump. She fills a couple buckets and leads a trail into the lab right to where she has them buried. She ignores the cries pleading for forgiveness.

William was gaining consciousness. Zorra says, "So, Willie boy, I'm told you're the only one that can give me information."

The smell of gasoline is consuming the building. William completely confused and nervous asks, "What's goin' on? What you doin'?"

Zorra has him gaze at the pile of Peligrosa and answers, "They're still alive and will be burning to death. You, however, I'll shoot in the head so that you'll die quickly, IF and only IF you tell me what I want to hear. Ricardo died in the building collapse during the night. The Peligrosa are no more. Where is Alejandro? Why did Ricardo want Alejandro and me?"

A scared William said, "I don't know where Alejandro is. I know he's not here. We lost all communication with Ricardo once the building collapsed. Last I knew at the church, Alejandro took out some men and drove away with the explosives. I got out of Dodge and came here to our rendezvous point. The original plan was to have both of you alive so he could get the bounty on your heads from Serpente in New York. That's it. That's all I know."

Zorra says, "He can't be...he had to survive. There is no way...," but deep down in her gut, she must be real. No sign of Alejandro anywhere. William could see Zorra getting angry.

"PLEASE don't kill me." William pleaded. "P-p-p-please let me go. Haven't I suffered enough from you?" he asked while pointing at his lack of eye and bleeding forehead then continues, "You've destroyed everything I got."

A very perturbed Zorra contemplating how he dared say she destroyed everything he had when that is exactly what had happened to her. The Peligrosa, from direct orders of the mayor, took away everything she held dear. Zorra starts punching William in the face as she yells, "You asshole! I'm Josefina Murrieta. You killed my family! You made me hear them burn! You killed Alejandro! You destroyed my life!" With every statement she is screaming, another fracture occurs to William's face. By the time she is done going all Rocky-on-a-frozen-rack-of-ribs, William's face resembles a mangled unrecognizable pile of bloody uncooked meatloaf. She just kneels there staring.

The shouts of the buried Peligrosa snap Zorra out of her bewilderment. She rises and slowly walks out of the warehouse. Zorra steps over two of the bodies that are holding the door open to the loading dock. She makes it to the Z and drives it closer to the gas-filled building. She opens the trunk to get one of the emergency road flares. After igniting it, she launches the flare into the building. The fumes burst into flames instantly blowing out the windows and sending a shockwave that tosses her back to the ground. Zorra gets back to her feet. She feels the heat, hears the screams, and smells the fire. She smiles but she is not happy. She goes back to the Z and heads back to One Bigler Avenue.

## CHAPTER 24

# IT'S BEEN A LONG WEEK

A new morning has begun. For the first time in years, the morning sky is starting to light up in the distance. Sunrise is not too far away. The miracle of an air current has brought many Perilous City residents out to the street to witness such beauty. Most of the alleyway dwellers haven't felt a ray of Sun in over a decade.

Construction vehicles such as backhoes and dump trucks are at the scene of destruction carefully moving the debris. All the public departments along with the hospitals have many people on the scene helping. Mercedes Downey and her Channel Six News crew are there, and she is talking with Captain Love.

Zorra parks her Z several blocks away for a couple of reasons; try to stay hidden and to avoid the police. By the time she gets close enough to the chaos she has been thanked numerous times by many residents for her good deeds, "Gracias Zorra. Muchas gracias."

Zorra can see everybody from the building she thinks she is hiding behind. The debris is immense. She knows there is no way anyone survived that collapse. As she is watching everything, she notices one New York-plated SUV, Zorra says, "Ahhh, Serpente's men. Let's see what they're up to," she creeps up closer toward them. Zorra scoots under the SUV and watches them as they approach.

Four of Serpente's men just finished walking from the congested activity. One of the New Yorkers is talking to Mr. Serpente on his cell phone. "Yes, Sir, all the loose ends are taken care of. There are no survivors and no connections. That treacherous Ricardo and his goons are no more. That Zorra and her partner caused such a ruckus the entire building collapsed. I just heard from Joe that the warehouse at the railyard is up in flames. There is no way anyone survived that building coming down. We'll just have to find another spot. We're leaving now. See you in a couple of days." He puts his phone away and the four men get into the vehicle and head off. Zorra holds tight until they drive away. She gets up and runs for the Z.

The Sun is up enough where the stealth of darkness is gone. She hears several more "gracias Zorra" along her way. Zorra unlocks the Z, gets in, and turns on the ignition. She is about to put it in drive when the passenger door opens. Mercedes Downey sits beside her and asks, "Where are we going?"

Zorra, surprisingly and annoyingly says, "I don't have time for this. Get out."

Mercedes stubbornly replies, "They're getting away."

Zorra pretends she has no clue who Mercedes is talking about, "Who?"

"The New Yorkers."

"What New Yorkers."

"Please, this is my job to notice things. You stick out like a sore thumb. You're lucky they didn't see you like I did. I'm not getting out."

"It's your funeral." Zorra speeds off to leave the city.

Mercedes asks her, "What's your plan? And who are the New Yorkers?"

Zorra smiles at Mercedes and then says, "You'll find out soon enough." She punches the accelerator and is on the interstate in no time. She catches up to the SUV. "Our exit is coming up. They'll follow me off. They think I'm dead too."

The Z pulls up next to the SUV. The driver looks out and glances at the ladies in the car. They read his lips clear as day, "It's that bitch Zorra, she ain't dead."

Zorra sticks up her middle finger at the driver, accelerates the Z more, and takes the exit following a state road east. Just like she thought the SUV was following them. Zorra lets the SUV catch up and she tells Mercedes to buckle up. Mercedes makes sure the belt is on and Zorra slams her brakes.

The driver of the SUV, not wanting to collide, swerves out of the way and goes off the road down the aqueduct embankment where he comes to a stop. Zorra tells Mercedes, "There are guns in the trunk," then darts out of the Z and runs towards the New Yorkers.

She gets to the edge of the embankment and slides down to confront them. All four, around six feet tall and buff, come out smiling at one another. Zorra knows what is coming. Like clockwork one of them states, "That's the little thing that has given this city so much trouble."

Zorra confidently says to them, "And now it's your turn." She goes to the driver and down blocks the gun out of his hand. Then grabs him behind the head and smashes his face with her elbow. She continues with a tiger paw to the face. She momentarily lets him go when she swings her elbow behind her knocking the other assailant back. Zorra brings the same elbow to the front and finishes off the driver smashing his face with the incoming elbow sending him flying into the side of the SUV.

The assailant behind Zorra approaches a little more wearily with his gun drawn. Zorra crescent kicks with her left leg knocking his right arm causing his gun to face a better location. She grabs his wrist and forearm. Keeping the gun pinned downward, Zorra comes up with a right-leg sidekick busting his jaw and sending him to the ground.

While Zorra was taking out both of Serpente's men on the driver's side, the other two made it around the SUV to see their buddies unconscious on the ground. Zorra crabwalks sideways quickly to her right and back fists the one near the hood right in the nose. She then grabs the back of his head with both hands and smacks him into the hood. While his eyes are getting all watery and his visibility is temporarily gone, Zorra heads for the fourth man.

The fourth attacker does not want any of this. He pulls out his gun and holds it tight with both hands and tells her not to move. Zorra drops to the ground, rolls under the SUV and comes out the other side. She uses the step rail and the roof rack on the other side and climbs on top of the vehicle. She looks down and the other man is bent over, looking under the SUV. "Too easy," she says then jumps down feet first onto his neck. He falls forward and busts his face on the driver's step rail. Definitely, she does not want them to gain consciousness and cause more havoc so she grabs one of their guns and puts a bullet into each of their heads.

Mercedes, whose leg is bandaged and is still healing from her gunshot wound, watched from the top. She asks with nervous concern, "Why did you execute them? What did they do?"

After removing their wallets, Zorra heads back up the embankment throwing the gun down, "Mercedes, there are things you don't know. These men, along with the mayor were funding the tyranny in our city."

"Don't you think you went too far? What about due process?"

"They were purchasing the heroin from Ricardo and his gang. They helped fund all the deaths, drugs, and kidnappings. That's all over now."

"What do you mean it's over?" Mercedes inquired.

"They were making the heroin at the railyard. That building is incinerated now. All the Peligrosa are gone. I saw to it. Ricardo went down with the mayor in the building. The citizens have a chance to prosper again. Everything in this city is set to get better. Well, almost everything. We lost a great man last night. Alejandro was in that building too. He's the one who sacrificed his life to bring the explosives to the building that was meant to take out the church. That's right! The church! Father O'Riley! Please check on him. I must get going."

Zorra points in the direction of the black SUV and says to Mercedes, "There's your ride back. The city needs you to help them get back on their feet. Please see to it that all the gold in the mayor's building makes it back to the people."

Now, Mercedes is thinking her cameraperson, Victoria, may be right about Zorra going too far. She doesn't want to upset her further, so she says what she feels she needs to say to get to safety, "what you have done for this city has been remarkable. The city needs you to help steer it in the right direction."

Climbing into the Z and tossing the wallets on the passenger seat, Zorra sighs to Mercedes and sadly tells her, "I don't exist in this city. It is no longer my home. I've got to go. There's nothing for me here." Mercedes starts walking towards Zorra when Zorra shoots her sharp glance, "There's no stopping me. Don't try. I'll ask you to do one thing for me."

Mercedes abruptly stops knowing not to press the issue, "What is it?"

"Please, you have to check on Father O'Riley and let him know I will be alright."

"Sure thing," but her reporting side continues when she asks, "but, where are you headed?"

Zorra releases a long breath and answers, "Not quite sure… I think my uncle would like me to visit an acquaintance, Mr. Serpente." Zorra starts the 350 Z convertible with its beautiful exhaust tune being heard. She opens the power roof, wishes she had a pair of sunglasses, and rides off into the sunrise.

The Adventure Begins